COVERT MISSION

TRIUMPH OVER ADVERSITY

LYNN SHANNON

CT
Creative Thoughts

COVERT MISSION

Copyright © 2022 by Lynn Balabanos

Published by Creative Thoughts, LLC

All rights reserved.

This book is a work of fiction. Names, characters, businesses, organizations, places, events and incidents either are the product of the author's imagination or are used factitiously. Any resemblance to actual persons, living or dead, events, or locales is entirely coincidental.

Cover design by Maria Spada.

Scripture appearing in this novel in whole or in part from THE HOLY BIBLE, NEW INTERNATIONAL VERSION®, NIV® Copyright © 1973, 1978, 1984, 2011 by Biblica, Inc.™ Used by permission. All rights reserved worldwide.

The eyes of the Lord are on the righteous,
and his ears are attentive to their cry.

Psalm 34:15

ONE

"There have been more death threats."

Willow Cassidy's heart skipped a beat. Opposite her, across the wide expanse of her desk, her uncle sat in a wing-back visitor's chair. His gaze was steely eyed, the hardened expression earned through three decades as a federal prosecutor. Scott Buchanan had a reputation for honesty, integrity, and a fierce devotion to fairness. He could also be stubborn and overbearingly protective, especially with his only blood relation left. Her.

"It's not the first time there have been threats against our family." Willow kept her tone steady. She didn't enjoy being on anyone's hit list, even if it was only in their imagination. From the furious look on her uncle's face, he shared her opinion. She offered him a reassuring smile. "We knew your campaign would place us in the spotlight."

In a surprise move Willow hadn't expected, Scott quit his job as a federal prosecutor last year and threw his hat into the ring to become a state senator. A series of scandals had plagued the district in the last two years—ones that had frustrated Scott immensely—but the elected senator held on. Jerry Randall intended to keep his job. He was running opposite Scott in the election, and things had turned decidedly uglier in recent months.

Willow folded her hands over her desk. "You don't have to come down to my office every single time there's been a new batch of threats. I'm being careful, Uncle Scott."

His expression remained grim. "This time things are different."

"How so?"

He removed several sheets of paper from the inner pocket of his suit jacket and laid them on her desk.

Willow inhaled sharply. Photographs of her had been taken serendipitously in different places: shopping at the grocery store, leaving her home, during a campaign event last week. The emails didn't include a message, but the photographs had a sniper's bull's-eye over her face. The threat was apparent.

A shiver raced down her spine. This wasn't the normal terrorizing message sent from an angry constituent. Someone had been following her. It was menacing and more than frightening, given the criminals her uncle had placed behind bars over the course of his career. "Do the police have any idea who sent these?"

"Chief Garcia is looking into the matter, of course, but there isn't much to go on." Scott leaned forward in his chair. "It's time for you to reconsider a full security detail."

Willow rose from her chair and walked to the broad expanse of glass separating her office from her staff. Blessed Hearts Youth Center was a nonprofit organization dedicated to helping teens in crisis. There was a 24-hour suicide line, trained counselors to provide support and guidance, tutors for school, sports events, and organized volunteer service activities. It was her passion project turned into reality through years of hard work and dedication. She'd struggled desperately as a teenager after losing her parents in a plane crash. Depression had nearly taken her life. Intervention by her grandmother—and later, Willow's faith—had pulled her through. She wanted to provide that opportunity for other kids struggling to find their way.

Expanding the youth center by adding an outdoor recreational area was the next move. Fundraising events were already underway after months of planning. Her calendar was full of activities, culminating with a final gala in two weeks.

Frustration bubbled inside her. How was Willow supposed to do everything she needed to with a full security detail trailing her? They would have to clear every store she entered and frisk any person she met with besides family. She knew. For a brief period of time, when her uncle was prosecuting a cartel member, he'd installed a full security detail around Willow. College hadn't been fun with three bodyguards tracking her every move.

"Doing my job would be impossible with a full security detail, Uncle Scott."

"You also can't do your job if you're dead."

Willow winced at his harsh retort. Scott's bluntness mirrored her mother's, a Buchanan trait that had served them well in business and in the courtroom, but not as much in family relationships. Her father had been a soft-spoken man with a quiet reserve of steel. Willow favored him in personality.

Scott sighed and softened his tone. "I know it'll be difficult, but we need to take these threats seriously."

"I am." She turned to face her uncle, unwilling to yield to his control. "But I'm not putting my life on hold because of some creepy emails. Expanding the youth center is important and it can't be done without donations." She smiled. "The trust fund only goes so far, you know."

She'd poured the inheritance from her parents into a charity trust fund with the youth center as a beneficiary. The money covered their operating costs, and would for years to come, but didn't allow for the kind of rapid expansion Willow wanted. For that, she needed donations.

The hint of a smile twitched Scott's lips. "Your parents would be very proud of the youth center, Willow." His expression turned grave again. "But you need protection."

"I have my driver, remember?" Bruce Snyder began working for her a few weeks ago at her uncle's insistence. He was a trained security guard who drove her back and forth to work. During the day, he kept an eye on the youth center.

Willow didn't like having a bodyguard at all, but her uncle's fears were legitimate considering the numerous threats sent to his campaign office over the last several months. Bruce was a compromise to prevent Scott from worrying.

"Most of my time is spent at my office or my home," she continued. "Both places are secure. I'm cautious, Uncle Scott, but I won't be bullied by a few nasty emails."

"Don't be foolish. These threats are directed at you specifically." Scott gestured to the pictures on her desk. "Bruce isn't enough. You need a full security detail."

Down the hall, Scott's own security detail stood like sentries waiting for battle. Their ramrod straight posture and ever-roaming eyes unnerved Willow. Yet another reason she didn't want a pack of bodyguards watching over her. It didn't make her feel safe, only trapped.

She resisted the urge to be petulant and took a deep breath to rein in her emotions. Scott was scared. She wouldn't talk him out of that, but Willow also refused to give in to it. "Let's give Chief Garcia a chance to investigate these threats. In the meantime, I'll be more vigilant about my surroundings."

He was quiet for a long moment. "You have your father's stubbornness."

She scoffed. "Buchanans aren't known for being weak-willed."

That comment earned her a smile. "No, we aren't." Scott rose, his gaze turning tender as he took a few steps in her direction. "Forgive me for being so pushy. I only want to keep you safe."

Warmth swelled in her chest. "I know."

She understood Scott's need to protect. While Willow favored her father in personality, she was a near replica of her mother physically. White-blonde hair, delicate features, and crystal-blue eyes. She was a living, breathing reminder of all Scott had lost. He'd been very close to his only sibling, and poured all of that love and grief into caring for Willow.

Scott's phone beeped. He pulled it from his pocket and frowned. "I have to go. Meeting with a donor."

"Best get to it then. You don't want to be late." Willow kissed his cheek.

Scott retrieved his jacket from the stand next to her door. "Call me if you need anything."

"Will do. Give my love to Kathryn."

Her aunt. Uncle Scott had married late in life. Kathryn was twenty years his junior, but smart and successful in her own right. She'd worked as a reporter and political correspondent before marrying Scott. Currently, she was his campaign manager.

Scott left with his bodyguards. Willow settled back into her leather chair with a sigh. Crisis averted. For now, anyway. She was under no illusions that her uncle would let the matter go.

The emails were still scattered across her desk. She studied each one. Based on the outfits she was wearing in the pictures, they'd been taken in the last week. Unnerving, especially since she hadn't sensed anyone watching her. Willow called her driver/bodyguard into her office.

Bruce entered and shut the door behind him. Probably unnecessary. Most of the staff had gone home for the day, given the late hour. It wasn't uncommon for her to be the first one there and the last to leave. She didn't have much of a life outside the youth center. Most of her friends, made in college, were scattered across the US. Dating was a distant memory. She'd come close to marrying her college sweetheart, but that had ended in disaster and heartbreak.

Willow showed Bruce the emails. "Have you noticed anyone watching us?"

He shook his head. His bald head shone in the fluorescent lighting. Bruce had the physique of a boxer with a barrel chest and thick neck. He also wore a perpetual scowl. It deepened as he studied the pictures. "Your uncle and

Chief Garcia already questioned me about these photos, ma'am. I never saw anyone suspicious hanging around."

It didn't surprise Willow to learn Scott had already questioned her bodyguard. He was probably considering firing the man as well, but Bruce couldn't be blamed for someone taking photographs with a long-view lens. His job was to prevent someone from approaching her with an immediate threat, not to spot a stalker.

Lightning streaked across the night sky beyond her window, followed by a clap of thunder. Willow jumped with the intensity of it. She laughed lightly. "The weather man promised there'd be a storm tonight. Guess he was right. We should head home before it gets too bad."

"Yes, ma'am."

Willow quickly gathered her things and shrugged on her jacket. Her gaze kept being drawn to the photographs on her desk. Popping open her briefcase, she shoved them inside next to her laptop. Maybe she'd review them later, try to pinpoint where and when they'd been taken. It could help Chief Garcia with the investigation.

She flipped off the lights to her office and then locked the office door. Bruce was sending a text when she met him in the hallway. He tucked his phone in his pocket and then guided her to a rear stairwell. For security purposes, her vehicle was parked in an adjacent staff lot instead of the main one. Wind howled when he pushed the door open. As they stepped outside, the skies opened. Rain pelted the asphalt in a fury.

Bruce opened an umbrella and turned. "Give me the keys and your things. I'll fetch the car so you don't have to walk in the rain."

Willow frowned but did as he asked. Her SUV was several rows down. Normally, she used the spot next to the door, but an afternoon meeting away from the office meant she'd lost the space to another employee. She'd also forgotten to take her umbrella with her this morning.

Bruce jogged across the parking lot. His form disappeared around the side of the vehicle. Willow tightened her coat around her midsection. The storm had brought a cold-front with it and the temperature dropped by the second. Rain pounded against the overhang covering the sidewalk. Wind pushed the drops sideways. They dampened her hair and iced her bare skin. Goosebumps pebbled on her neck.

What was Bruce doing? Why was it taking him so long to start the car?

She fisted her hands. Her breath formed puffs in the night air. Willow peered through the curtain of rain, trying to see what Bruce was doing, but it was impossible. A creepy sensation washed over her. She glanced behind her. The door to the building was closed. It automatically locked and her master key was on the same key chain as her SUV. Going back inside wouldn't be possible. And her cell phone was in her briefcase, which Bruce had taken with him.

Pulling a can of pepper spray from her jacket pocket, Willow eased to the end of the sidewalk. She could go around the side of the building to the front, but she'd have to pass by her vehicle anyway. And would she abandon Bruce if there was trouble? Could she honestly forgive herself if something happened to him?

The answer was no. The man had a wife and a little girl. Even if he didn't, it wasn't in her nature to run away from a potential problem. Not anymore. Doing so as a teenager had nearly destroyed her.

Willow stepped off the sidewalk and into the rain. It soaked her instantly. She blinked rapidly to clear her eyelashes of the droplets and moved forward. Darkness shrouded the parking lot. The lights from the building weren't enough given the cloud cover caused by the storm. She approached the vehicle. "Bruce?"

It was nothing. Maybe Bruce was on a phone call. She'd be laughing at her silliness in a few minutes. "Bruce?"

He didn't answer.

Willow circled the bumper of her SUV and stopped short. The driver's side door hung open. Her briefcase was nowhere to be seen, and neither was her bodyguard. The hair on the back of her neck stood up. Fear cramped her stomach. Some deep instinct urged her to take a step back.

Wrong. Something was very wrong.

She whirled. A large form came out of the darkness, heading straight for her. It was a man in a ski mask.

Willow screamed. She hit the button on her pepper spray, but the attacker knocked it from her hand before the aerosol was freed from the can. It slipped from her grasp and clattered against the ground.

Leaving her defenseless.

TWO

Logan Keller gripped the steering wheel of his Jeep Grand Cherokee. Exhaustion seeped into every muscle in his body. He'd worked as a paramedic and pulled a double shift. Years spent in the military had taught him how to manage periods of little rest. An injury had ruined his career in the Air Force, but he was blessed to have a similar civilian job.

Right now, he wanted two things: a shower and his bed. Unfortunately, he'd have to wait for both. His niece, Mia, had skipped school again this afternoon. Her third time this month. Logan suspected some of the new friends she'd made recently were smoking marijuana and drinking alcohol. Mia was spiraling after losing her parents in a car crash last year. Heart-to-hearts hadn't worked. Neither had punishments or restrictions. He was at his wit's end. And terrified. No amount of military training had prepared him for parenting a grieving and distraught fifteen-year-old.

What were you thinking, Sean?

Logan's older brother had been the perfect dad.

Responsible and bighearted, with an easy smile and a kind word for everyone. His shoes were impossible to fill. Mia knew it too. The kid was brilliant. A little too smart for her own good, truth be told.

Their connection had been infrequent while she was growing up. Logan had spent most of the time she was alive serving in the Air Force. Trips home to Knoxville had been for short periods of time, to see his brother's family and their parents. Mia had always been there, first as a tiny infant and then later a kid he bought awesome Christmas presents for. Logan had always loved her. That was never in question. But he didn't *know* her, not like her parents did.

And then the car crash happened.

Logan hadn't realized he was Mia's appointed guardian until after his brother and sister-in-law died. He'd always just assumed his parents would care for her. In retrospect, it'd been a foolish thought. Their father had suffered from two heart attacks in the last several years, their mother a bout with colon cancer. They weren't spring chickens. Mia was only fifteen. She needed a parent who could see her through high school and well beyond. Sean's wife had been an orphan without family.

The only one left was Logan. He had help from his parents, thank God. They watched Mia on the days he had to work and provided guidance, but ultimately, he was in charge. He became a parent overnight. The responsibility pressing down on Logan's shoulders, coupled with the grief of losing his only sibling, was crushing. He felt lost.

Rain battered his windshield, fast and furious. The wipers had trouble keeping up. Logan kept his speed slower than normal as he drove through town. His mother had told him about a charity for troubled teens months ago. Initially when Mia started acting up, he'd thought they would get through it as a family, but that approach wasn't working. Things were progressively getting worse. If he didn't get a grasp on her now, Logan feared where she would end up. Drug addicted? In prison? Dead?

None of those were options he was willing to accept.

Today, between emergency calls at work, he'd done research on Blessed Hearts Youth Center. Its mission was to aid teens in crisis. They had counselors on staff, as well as tutors for school. Logan had also spoken to his pastor about it. The man had praised the center and the director, Willow Cassidy.

It was late, and the chances of finding anyone at the charity were slim, but Logan didn't want to put it off. Mia needed help. The sooner, the better.

The youth center came into view. It was a red bricked building next door to a barber shop. On the opposite side of the building was farmland butting up against a state park. Logan slowed to turn into the parking lot, relieved to find lights glowing inside the building. This might not have been a futile errand after all. Some staff were still inside.

He parked his vehicle before grabbing an umbrella. Rain pelted him sideways as he opened his truck door. It chilled his skin.

A scream echoed across the lot.

Logan gripped his umbrella tighter. That'd come from the side of the building. Before he could even register the movement, his feet were already pounding against the pavement. Water soaked his boots and the legs of his paramedic uniform. Mentally, he wished for his handgun. It was locked up in a safe at home since he couldn't carry it while working. Knoxville, Texas was a safe town, but there were still riffraff and dangerous situations.

Training slowed his steps as he approached the corner of the building. The side lot was darker than the main one. His gaze swept across several lights that'd either burned out or been disabled. A lone SUV sat several meters away. The sounds of a scuffle reached his ears, followed by another scream that was cut off abruptly.

He charged ahead. It was reckless to do so. The assailant could have a gun, but that'd been a woman's scream. He couldn't leave her alone and defenseless. Not when he had military training and a knowledge of combat. It wasn't in him to shy away from confrontation.

Logan rounded the backend of the SUV. In seconds, his brain processed the scene in front of him. A man in black clothing was attempting to subdue a woman. She was fighting like a wild cat, her arms and legs moving too quickly for the attacker to get a good hold on her. Without hesitation, Logan charged.

He collided with the other man and they flew across the parking lot. Hard cement smashed against Logan's shoulder and hip. He barely felt the pain. His hands balled into fists and he landed a punch across the guy's jaw. The man responded by clocking him upside the head with the butt of a gun. Stars exploded across his vision. He toppled to the side. Before he could recover, the assailant was on his feet. He bolted across the grassy divide and disappeared down an alley.

Rage churning his insides, Logan scrambled to his feet.

He wanted to pursue the criminal with every fiber in his being, but his first goal had to be the woman. She could be seriously hurt. He spun on his heel, and his heart clenched tight when he caught sight of her bowled over on the ground.

Logan rushed to her side. "My name is Logan Keller and I work for the Knoxville EMS. Are you hurt?"

"No, it's not serious." She struggled to her feet, using the open driver's side door as a crutch. "My bodyguard is missing. We need to find him."

Bodyguard? That created a dozen questions in Logan's mind, but he held them back. It was hard to access her condition in the dark parking lot. She was clutching her shoulder with the opposite hand. Hair clung to her forehead. They were both soaked to the bone. He needed to get her someplace warm and dry. Then the police had to be called. If she needed a bodyguard, then chances were her assailant hadn't gone far.

Logan gently took her elbow. "Let's get you inside and then I'll come back to—"

She shrugged him off. "No. Now." Her voice trembled. "Please... Logan, was it? My name is Willow. We don't know each other, but I promise, I'm okay. My bodyguard came ahead of me to the SUV so I wouldn't have to walk in the rain. But then he never started the car. When I came out to check on him, that guy attacked me. I'm afraid..."

Willow was worried her bodyguard was seriously injured. Or dead. It wasn't unreasonable. Logan knew the smart thing to do was to take her inside, but he sensed she'd fight him every step of the way. Or run off to find the bodyguard herself.

He jerked his chin toward the SUV. "Get inside the vehicle and lock the doors. I'll look for your bodyguard. Call 911 while you're in there, and if anyone approaches the SUV before I come back, lay on the horn."

She opened her mouth to protest and he shook his head to cut her off. "Unless you're a cop or military, you'd only be in my way." He softened his tone. "Trust me, I know what I'm doing."

This time, Willow nodded. She scrambled into the SUV. Logan spotted a utility knife in the side pocket. The blade was jagged and used to cut through a seat belt. The other end had a point for smashing windows to aid escape if the SUV was submerged. He grabbed it and removed the knife from its sheath. It wouldn't stop a bullet, but it gave him a better chance than merely using his fists.

Logan slammed the door shut and waited until the locks snicked into place. The rain was still coming down in sheets. His uniform was plastered to his body. Warm blood seeped from his head wound and a dull ache pulsed from the place where he'd been hit with the attacker's gun. He blocked all of that out. Instead, he moved around the front of the vehicle, listening for any sound of the bodyguard.

A lump of darkness caught his attention. It was near the divider, close to the alley.

Logan approached cautiously, his fingers wrapped around the grip of the knife. "Sir, are you okay?"

The man didn't answer.

Logan continued, his gaze sweeping the immediate area before focusing back on the form lying on the ground. "Sir, answer me. Are you okay?"

Nothing. A chilling thought skittered through Logan's mind. The man was unnaturally still.

A prayer lifted from Logan's heart as he closed the distance between them. He kept the knife ready even as he bent down and placed two fingers at the bodyguard's throat.

No pulse. He was dead.

The SUV's horn blared.

THREE

Willow wrapped her arms around her midsection to keep her hands from shaking. She'd changed out of her soaking wet clothes into a spare outfit kept in the office for emergencies, but nothing could take away the goosebumps skating across her skin. The parking lot beyond the glass window of her office was full of police cars. Strobing red-and-blue lights flashed across the pavement and bounced off the neighboring buildings. Her bodyguard was dead. Shot. Murdered by the same man who'd attacked her. It was terrifying.

A knock on the open doorframe jolted her. Willow spun, her hands immediately balling into fists. It took a few seconds to register the man standing in her doorway. Logan Keller. Like her, he'd changed out of his wet clothing into a dry paramedic's uniform. The fabric molded to the broad width of his shoulders before narrowing to his waist. His dark hair was cut short in a military fashion. Thick brows arched over piercing eyes the color of rich chocolate. The curve of his jawline was well-defined, leading to a firm chin and masculine lips. He was, as her aunt would put it, sinfully handsome.

Logan raised one of his hands in the classic sign of surrender. The other held a medic's bag. "Sorry, I didn't mean to startle you."

She let out a breath and lowered her fists. She didn't know whether to laugh or cry. Of course the killer wouldn't knock on her office door. "It's not you. I'm jumpy."

His eyes darkened with sympathy. "That's not surprising, all things considered. I assume you had a bodyguard because you're in some kind of danger."

It was an assertion, but his voice rose at the end as if he was asking a question. Willow nodded in reply. "My uncle is Scott Buchanan. He's currently campaigning to become a state senator. There have been threats made against our family. Against me." Willow swallowed hard, her gaze once again drifting to the commotion happening in the parking lot. "The police chief took my statement and asked me to wait while he conducted an initial investigation. I'm hoping they'll catch the guy tonight."

It would go a long way to easing the fear chilling her core. A fresh wave of guilt followed the thought. How could Willow even think about herself? She was alive and breathing. Her bodyguard was dead. Hot tears pressed against the back of her eyelids. Her uncle couldn't have installed a security team tonight even if Willow had agreed to one, but that fact was little comfort. "Bruce. That's my bodyguard. I didn't know him well, but he has a wife and child. A daughter. She's five." A little girl was going to wake up tomorrow to find her entire world changed forever. Willow knew intimately what that was like. Her own parents had been taken from this world far too soon. "I need to call them—"

"I'm sure Chief Garcia will want to notify the family." Logan's tone was soothing. His boots were silent against the carpet as he came to stand next to her. "Mind if I look at your injuries? The chief mentioned you refused medical treatment, but it's not wise to leave those cuts untreated. Infection can set in faster than people think."

Her hand fluttered to the scrape along her neck. After Logan went to search for her bodyguard, the attacker had circled back and broken the driver's side window on Willow's SUV. The glass had cut her. She'd barely felt the injury when she laid on the horn, but now it throbbed painfully. There was another cut on her shin, along with a multitude of bruises that would ache tomorrow. The first aid kit was in the office somewhere, but she didn't have the energy to search for it.

She tore her gaze away from the window to study the man standing at her side. Everything about him, from the patches on his uniform to the powerful line of his back, eluded confidence. They were strangers and Willow was normally slow to trust, but inexplicably nodded. "Okay."

Logan smiled slightly and gestured to her desk chair. "Have a seat."

She did as he instructed. Logan set his heavy bag on her desk and opened it. His profile was as arresting as the rest of him. She watched, fascinated, as he removed antibacterial wipes. They were so flimsy in his strong hands. A rush of awareness and attraction swept over her.

Heat infused Willow's cheeks. What business did she have thinking about her handsome rescuer when another man lay dead in the parking lot just beyond her office windows? A fresh wave of guilt swept over her, followed by a shiver of fear. Then she understood. Logan was a distraction. A whim to help Willow get through this terrible night so she could go home and cry herself to sleep.

She mentally gave herself a shake. The only way through this horrible event was by facing it head on. It's what had gotten her through other difficult chapters in her life. Willow cleared her throat. "I haven't properly thanked you for what you did. It was brave. You saved my life."

He lifted a shoulder in a half-shrug. "I did what anyone would have."

"I think we both know that's not true."

Logan met her gaze briefly before ripping open an antibacterial wipe and focusing on the scrape along her neck. "This may sting."

His touch was gentle, and although the medicine burned, it wasn't overly painful. Willow did her best to ignore the butterflies flitting in her stomach. Especially when Logan reached up with one gloved hand and gently turned her head to have better access to her neck. His gaze was intense, and once again, Willow found her thoughts drifting to strange places. What would it be like to have the complete focus of a man like Logan? To feel the full weight of his attention solely on her?

Good grief, she was losing her mind! Willow prided herself on logic and caution. She'd allowed her heart to overrule her head once with disastrous results. Senior year of college, she met Mike Jensen. He was smart and funny and swept Willow off her feet. Their relationship was headed toward marriage—until she overheard Mike saying to a friend that he was dating Willow for her money and connections.

The truth had ripped her to shreds. Layered over the heartbreak was realizing she'd ignored any sign of Mike's true intentions until it was glaringly obvious. Willow had been in love. It'd blinded her, and she vowed to never play the fool again. So far, she'd kept that promise. Her dating life was almost nonexistent because it was incredibly difficult to sort out the men who were genuinely interested in her versus in her money. Trust didn't come easily to her anymore.

"I was coming to see you," Logan said, pulling Willow from her ruminations. "Tonight. That's why I was in the parking lot." He released her chin and took a step back. "God put me in the right place at the right time. I'm glad He did and that you're okay. I'm sorry about your bodyguard."

There was a lot to process, but one aspect of his statement surprised her. Willow tilted her head. "What were you coming to see me about?"

"It's not important—"

"No, please." Willow flipped her bangs out of her eyes and tucked the ends behind her ear. "Don't hold back because of what happened tonight. Distract me. Tell me why you were coming to see me."

He bent down to examine the wound on her shin, visible under the hem of her pencil skirt, and then grabbed a new antibacterial wipe. "My niece is getting into trouble. Mia lost her parents last year in a car accident, and now I'm her guardian. It hasn't been easy. She's been acting out since her parents died. We've gone from a bad attitude to skipping school and hanging with the wrong crowd. She's failing several subjects. Nothing I say seems to get through to her."

"She's hurting." Willow felt a pang of sympathy for the young woman. "How old is she?"

"Fifteen."

"Tough age."

Logan snorted. "Tell me about it." He swiped at the scrape on Willow's calf. "What do I do? How do I help her?"

His voice held a note of desperation. It was touching to see this hardened man who'd faced down a murderer with such bravery be bold enough to ask for help for his niece. Mia, whether or not she realized it, was fortunate to have Logan in her corner. Willow's esteem for him went up another notch. "We have counselors on staff who can talk to her. Mia may need a safe place to discuss the feelings she's experiencing."

"Are you saying she can't talk to me? Or my parents?" Logan scowled. "We're her family."

"And all of you are grieving." Willow kept her tone gentle and nonconfrontational. She had no desire to make him feel like he wasn't doing a good job as a guardian. "Mia may worry that talking will drudge up painful feelings for you. It sounds funny, I know, but she could be trying to protect you."

He tossed the wipe in the trash can and peeled off his gloves, adding them to the pile as well. From the furrow of his brow, Willow could tell he was mulling over her observation. She gave him a moment and then added, "Bring her to the center. Explain to Mia that this is a place she can receive tutoring for her failing grades. My staff is excellent.

They will encourage her to talk to our counselors and then we can go from there."

"I don't think Mia gives a fig about her grades."

"Was she a good student before her parents died?"

He nodded. "Straight As."

"Then she cares. It's just a matter of tapping into it." Willow paused and then rose from her chair. "If you can't get her to the center, then I'll come to your house and talk to her. I went through a very difficult period after losing my parents in a plane crash at thirteen. It's the reason I started the youth center." Without thinking, she placed a hand on his arm. "We'll get through to her."

Logan's gaze swung to hers. This close, Willow could see the richer brown flecks in his eyes. The spark of attraction she'd experienced earlier burst into flame. All at once, she became increasingly aware of his closeness. The scent of his aftershave—something warm and masculine—mingled with the scent of his damp hair. Her heart skipped a beat.

Footsteps in the hall broke the spell. Willow yanked her hand back and stepped away from Logan. She avoided his gaze, instead focusing on the open office door. Moments later, Chief Sam Garcia entered the room. His police uniform was speckled with water spots from the rain and a cowboy hat covered his salt-and-pepper hair.

Willow knew the chief well. He'd taken over the Knoxville police department several years ago. As a result, he worked closely with her uncle whenever a case involved federal charges. The two men had formed a friendship. The chief and his wife were frequent guests at parties or for summer BBQs. She'd always like Chief Garcia. He was thorough and dedicated to keeping the citizens of their town safe.

The scowl drawing down his brows sent a hard dose of reality coursing through her veins. Her knees weakened. "You didn't catch the attacker, did you?"

Chief Garcia shook his head. "Not yet. But I've got every available lawman in the state searching based on the description you both provided." His gaze went toward Logan. "I'd like to ask a few follow-up questions of you both, if you don't mind." He waited for them to nod and then pulled a pad from the front pocket of his shirt. "Willow, can you describe the perpetrator again for me?"

"I didn't get a good look at him. He was taller than me, about 6'1 or 6'2. Dark clothes. He wore a ski mask." A shiver racked her body. "I couldn't even tell you his ethnicity."

"And he didn't speak to you at all?"

She shook her head. "No. During the initial attack, he tried to grab me, but I fought him. After Logan left to find..." Willow's throat closed at the thought of her dead bodyguard. She took a deep breath to steady her emotions. "The attacker circled back around and broke my window with the butt of his gun. I pressed on the horn and Logan came running."

"The perpetrator ran westward down the alley," Logan added. "Same direction I saw him go the first time. My guess is he had a vehicle nearby and used that to escape."

A thought wiggled its way past the trembles threatening to take over Willow's body. "The attacker had a gun. He killed my bodyguard. Why didn't he shoot me?"

"It's too early in the investigation for me to say."

A commotion in the hallway caught Willow's attention. Through the glass wall of her office, she spotted her uncle. He was flanked by his bodyguards and several police officers. She'd called Uncle Scott after the attack, primarily to reassure him. From the force of his steps and the dark look on his face, he hadn't been convinced by their conversation.

He entered the office and beelined straight for Willow, wrapping her in his embrace. "Thank God, you're okay."

She hugged her uncle back. The familiar warmth of his embrace instantly comforted her, even as a pang of loneliness wriggled its way through. What she would give to have her father here now. Dad always had the right words to make her feel safe. "I'm fine, Uncle Scott. There was no need for you to come down here."

"There's every need." He backed away but kept his hands lightly on her arms. "I have information about the attack. Things are worse than we thought."

FOUR

The next morning, Logan stifled a yawn as he poured another cup of coffee. He hadn't slept easy last night. After Willow's uncle arrived, he'd asked to speak to the police chief and his niece alone. An understandable request. Whatever he'd uncovered about the attack should be kept within law enforcement and the family.

Still, Logan worried. He had every intention of following up with Chief Garcia about the matter later on this morning. Willow Cassidy was little more than a stranger, but something about the gorgeous blonde tugged at his protective instincts. Her vulnerability? Her kind offer to help with his niece? Logan couldn't quite piece it together, but the feeling was there all the same. He wanted to make sure she was safe.

Shoving thoughts of Willow aside, Logan checked his watch. Irritation flared. He went to the base of the stairs. "Mia, hurry up. You're going to be late for school."

A door slammed in response. Moments later, boots clomped down the stairs. Mia was dressed in ripped black jeans, a matching black T-shirt, and heavy combat boots. Her hair was braided on one side close to her scalp, while the other half was left to mingle with the multitude of earrings dangling from her lobe. Black eyeliner and dark lipstick completed the morose outfit. It matched the deep scowl on her face.

Logan arched a brow. "Where did those clothes come from?"

He certainly hadn't bought them, and he doubted his parents had. The makeup either.

Mia hauled her backpack higher on one shoulder. Her muscles stiffened, and she glared at him. "They used to be Debbie's. She cleaned out her closet and gave me some stuff that didn't fit her anymore."

Great. Debbie was seventeen and attended the same school as Mia. She was a failing senior on a fast track to trouble. One of the many new friends Mia had made recently.

His niece marched into the kitchen and threw her backpack on a chair. Logan battled the urge to order Mia to remove the makeup. Where was the beautiful young woman who loved pastel colors and a fresh face? Overnight, she'd disappeared. If Mia were in her twenties and dressed this way, Logan wouldn't say a word. She'd be a grown woman able to make her own choices. But for a fifteen-year-old… it felt like she was trying too hard to be older than her years. And it didn't fit with her true personality. Mia had been a bubbling, bright, positive ray of light before her parents died. This dark look seemed to represent everything hidden inside. It scared him.

Instead of confronting that battle, he offered Mia a plate

of scrambled eggs and bacon. She waved it away and popped open the pantry before grabbing a breakfast bar. "I'll walk to school."

That was a no-go. Mia couldn't be trusted to make it there. Skipping class had become a new pastime. Logan shot her a warning look. "I'll drive you."

She rolled her eyes. "Whatever."

Logan gritted his teeth and snagged his car keys from the door. "Let's go."

Mia dutifully followed him to the garage and climbed into the passenger seat before slamming the door with more force than was necessary. She crossed her arms over her chest, the scowl permanently etched across her features. Mia's bad attitude was like an elephant in the Jeep with them. It sucked all the air out of the vehicle and left him feeling unsettled. Uncertain. Logan didn't like it.

He was a military trained soldier, for crying out loud. He'd parachuted into combat zones to rescue injured men. Been shot and survived. Faced life-and-death situations daily as a paramedic. But one angry and heartbroken teen left him floundering.

He backed out of the drive and set a course for the school. It was only six blocks away. "What time is detention over today?"

"Five." The look she shot him and the tone in her voice screamed idiot. "Same as every other time." Mia glowered. "I can get home on my own. No one needs to pick me up. I'm sick of everyone treating me like a child."

"Then stop acting like one. Trust is earned, Mia, and you've destroyed our ability to believe anything you say." Logan kept his tone even. Yelling wouldn't help matters.

"You can remedy the situation by following the rules. It's up to you how we handle things. Until then, Nana or I will pick you up."

She rolled her eyes again but said nothing. Logan joined the long line of cars snaking their way to the school's drop-off area. "Nana would like your help with the town's Thanksgiving food drive. It's a good opportunity to earn extra credit by doing community service work. Your principal, Mrs. Jackson, has signed off already."

"Nice of everyone to go around making plans for me. Did any of you think I might not want to spend my time hauling around boxes and sorting cans of pumpkin pie filling?" She tossed her hair over her shoulder. "I'm not doing it."

"You're failing, Mia. Do you want to repeat your sophomore year?" Logan fought for patience. "Is that what your parents would have wanted?"

"My parents are dead, so frankly, I don't think they care anymore."

Her response was a knife wound to Logan's chest. He inhaled sharply. "I know you're hurting—"

"Save it, Uncle Logan. I've already heard all the God mumbo-jumbo from Nana. The Lord is watching over me and prayer is the way through my grief." She popped open the passenger-side door. "It's all a load of baloney. God took my parents from me. The way I see it, He's not doing me any favors."

With those parting words, she slammed the car door shut and marched toward the school building. Her shoulders were hunched, hands stuffed in the pockets of her jeans. Mia looked lost. In pain. Achingly lonely.

Logan leaned against the headrest and closed his eyes. "What do I do, Lord? How do I get through to her?"

A car horn blared in response to his prayer. Logan popped his eyes open and waved at the vehicle behind him before pulling away from the curb. The drive home felt desolate. Nothing Logan or his parents said seemed to ease Mia's pain. Anger was a normal part of the grieving process, but his niece was holding on to it with a ferocious determination. As if it was the only thing holding her together.

Maybe it was. Logan himself hadn't truly grieved his brother and sister-in-law. He'd never cried over their deaths or allowed himself to absorb the pain of their loss. There hadn't been time. Taking care of Mia, going to work, putting one foot in front of the other every day took so much energy... he couldn't fall apart. But once again, Logan was struck with the notion that he was failing his niece massively.

As he turned onto his street, any thoughts of Mia fled. An unfamiliar SUV was parked in front of his house. Logan's gaze shot to his front porch and his pulse skipped a beat. Willow. She was dressed professionally in a pants suit that hugged every curve and heels that added several inches to her petite frame. Last night, her hair had been rumpled and damp from the rain. Today, the strands shone in the sunshine, cut into a face-framing bob with bangs that skimmed her eyes. At her side on the porch was a muscular man in a suit and sunglasses. Another bodyguard stood next to the vehicle.

Willow looked every inch of the wealthy socialite she was. A quick internet search last night had answered a lot of Logan's questions about the woman he rescued. She was the only grandchild of Jacob and Eloise Buchanan, a couple who'd made their fortune by starting a grocery store chain that'd expanded across the US. Willow's parents took over the family business, but it was sold after they died in a plane crash. She'd only been thirteen at the time. Her uncle, Scott Buchanan, a former federal prosecutor, took Willow in and raised her. He was married, but had no children of his own.

The Buchanans were the richest people in Knoxville and one of the wealthiest families in Texas. Their connections and influence were far-reaching. Scott's run for state senator was the beginning of his political career, but Logan suspected it wouldn't be the end. He was the type who would advance quickly in that world.

The SUV's rear door opened and Scott stepped out of the vehicle, talking on the phone. He said a final few words, hung up, and tucked the device in the pocket of his suit. His hair was combed away from his face, his wingtips shoes shined to perfection, but nothing could erase the lines of worry bracketing his mouth. He joined Willow on the porch.

Logan parked his Jeep and got out, crossing the yard on long strides. "Hello."

Willow greeted him with a soft smile. "Hi, Logan. Sorry to drop by unannounced." She thrust the gift basket in her hands toward him. "We wanted to thank you again in person for last night."

"We also need to speak to you," Scott added. "Do you mind if we come in?"

Willow shot her uncle a questioning look as Logan took the basket from her. It was heavy with expensive cheeses, fancy crackers, flavored chocolates, and other things he couldn't name. He juggled it while opening the front door. "Of course. Please come in. Would you like some coffee?"

"No, thank you." Scott gestured for Willow to go inside and then he followed her over the threshold. "Harry, we'll be a few minutes. Stay here."

The bodyguard on the porch nodded. Logan shut the door. Mia's discarded hoodie hung from the recliner and an empty soda can sat on the coffee table. The kitchen, visible from the living room, wasn't much better. Two dirty skillets —one from the eggs, another from the bacon—sat on the stove top. Dishes were piled in the sink. Embarrassment heated Logan's neck as he tossed Mia's hoodie in the laundry room. "Sorry. I wasn't expecting guests."

"No, please." Willow waved her hand dismissively, shooting her uncle another questioning look. "We're the ones intruding." She crossed to the piano near the window. "Do you play?"

"Yes, but Mia is the real musician in the family. She started years ago and played for the church until..." Her parents died. Logan didn't want to talk about that right now. "We haven't lived here long. The house is a rental. I didn't have much stuff before moving to Knoxville since I was in the Air Force. The military shifts you from base to base. You learn how to live out of a duffel bag. Any furniture you collect is cheap and often left behind to avoid having to move it."

Logan glanced around, seeing the space from the view of an outsider. It was a touch sad. A cheap couch was paired with a recliner and a chipped wooden coffee table. He hadn't bothered to hang photos, and the bookshelf in the corner only held a few novels.

Old habits died hard. But for Mia's sake, he should've made more effort. Logan added it to the increasing stack of failures racking up since taking over as her guardian. He gestured to the piano. "That was the one thing Mia asked to bring when we moved."

Everything else was sold when his brother's house went into foreclosure. Mia's parents had been fantastic in raising her, but not as good with their finances. Logan shook off the thought. He turned to Scott. "What did you need to discuss with me?"

Scott cleared his throat and extended his hand toward Logan. "First, I want to say thank you for what you did yesterday. I owe you a debt of gratitude, Mr. Keller. One that can never be fully repaid, but that won't stop me from trying."

"I appreciate the sentiment, sir, but there's no need for it. And please, call me Logan."

The older man nodded. "Scott." He released Logan's hand and stepped back. "I have a favor to ask of you. It involves Willow and the threat against her."

From the furrow of Willow's brow, she had no idea where her uncle was going with the conversation. Logan gestured to his couch. "Please have a seat. I'm happy to help in any way I can."

"Uncle Scott, I don't think we need to involve Logan any more than he already has—"

"There's every need." Scott turned to Logan. "Last night, I suspected Willow's bodyguard was paid to look the other way when she was attacked. Something must've gone wrong because he was killed, but the fact remains. Bruce was involved."

"How can you be certain?"

"Another employee tipped me off. Bruce had been bragging about coming into some cash. This morning, I received confirmation of my suspicions. A sizeable sum of money was transferred to his account two days ago and his wife doesn't know where it came from." His lips flattened into a thin line. "Each man in my security staff is thoroughly vetted. If one can be bought, then others can as well. We can't trust anyone."

His words rocked Logan to his core. That Willow had been attacked at all was horrifying, but to be betrayed by her own bodyguard was unforgivable. Scott was wise to be cautious. Whoever was behind these attacks had money, enough to convince a man to betray his duty. It could happen again. "Do you have any idea who is behind these attacks?"

Scott breathed out. "No. I spent thirty years as a federal prosecutor and made many enemies along the way. Drug dealers, high-level cartel leaders, and murderers. I've put together a list of criminals who could have the funds and resources to pull something like this off, but it'll take time to track them down." He scraped a hand through his hair, mussing the previously perfect strands. "Chief Garcia informed me last night that you have a group of friends who've come to the aid of several individuals in trouble. He's nicknamed you guys The Special Forces."

"Has he?" Logan arched his brows. "I didn't know that."

The moniker fit. Logan was part of an informal support group for veterans. It'd become a tight-knit circle of six guys. They met every Wednesday at a local diner and discussed the challenges each of them faced since leaving the military.

Over the last few years, they'd also become embroiled in some serious cases involving murder, kidnapping, and corruption. Several of his teammates had fallen in love along the way. Logan and his buddy Walker were the only ones still firmly entrenched in bachelorhood.

Being single was fine with Logan. Especially considering the pile of family drama he was currently dealing with. The last thing on his mind was finding a romantic relationship.

Scott fixed his steely gaze on Logan. "I'd like to hire you to protect Willow. Chief Garcia has vouched for you, and I've known him for years. He's never steered me wrong in the past. I need someone I can trust to keep her safe."

"Hold on." Willow stepped forward, making her presence known. "Sorry, Logan, I didn't know this was going to be a topic of conversation. Uncle Scott, we already discussed a security detail, which I've agreed to. Logan has a full-time job. He can't spend every waking minute following me around."

"I have a mountain of vacation days that need to be taken. My job isn't a problem." Logan leaned forward. "But Willow's right. I can't protect her every minute. I can ask my friends to help, but each of them has their own lives. There's no guarantee they'll agree."

"Understood. I'll still hire extra security for Willow, but the threat against her is serious. I want someone on the inside, working undercover, as a backup bodyguard. That way, if a member of the security team is compromised again, Willow still has protection."

"Undercover? How would that work?"

Scott opened his briefcase and pulled out a newspaper,

setting it on the coffee table. On the front page was a grainy photograph of Logan carrying Willow in the rain after the attack last night. The headline read: LOCAL PARA-MEDIC SAVES SENATE CANDIDATE'S NIECE.

Willow snatched up the paper. "What on earth? Where did they get this picture?"

"Security camera on the backside of the barbershop. Unfortunately, it didn't have a visual of your SUV, so we don't have footage of the attack. This image was captured as Logan carried you into the youth center. The article will run tomorrow morning. This was an advanced copy sent to my office as a heads-up." Scott steepled his fingers. "I suggest we use this story to our advantage. We'll simply let it leak that you and Logan began dating. As your boyfriend, it would make perfect sense for him to spend time with you, especially at social events when you're the most vulnerable to an attack."

"That's... that's..." Willow sputtered. Her cheeks heated as she glared at her uncle. "That's a terrible idea. The worst." She seemed to recognize how awful her words could be interpreted, because she turned to Logan. "No offense. It's not you."

"None taken." He wasn't thrilled to be her undercover boyfriend either, but he couldn't argue with Scott's logic. Hiding in plain sight as Willow's boyfriend gave her an extra layer of protection. "What you're asking would entail lying to people."

"It would mean lying to everyone, including your family and friends. No one outside of this room can know the relationship is fake." Scott gestured to the newspaper clutched in Willow's hand. "Newspaper reporters are going to be all over this story. We can't afford to have anything leaked to the press."

Willow shook her head. "No, Uncle Scott. I won't do that."

"It's the best way to protect you." His tone brooked no argument. "I understand lying goes against your moral code, but sometimes such matters are required. The only other option is to sequester you away in a safe house. But I don't know how long the investigation will take and it would mean canceling your fundraising efforts."

"What fundraising efforts?" Logan injected.

"I'm raising money to build an outdoor recreational area for Blessed Hearts. We've been planning the events for months. Canceling them is impossible. Tickets for the gala and the baseball game between our teens and the fire department have already been sold." She set the paper down on the coffee table. "Not to mention that I'm the face of the youth center. It's important for me to shake hands with donors and do publicity for the events. I can't simply disappear from my life for an indeterminate period."

Willow's dedication to her youth center tugged at Logan's heartstrings. It also placed her in danger. Before he could even rationally think the decision through, Logan said, "Then your uncle is right. You need protection."

Her mouth dropped open. "You aren't seriously entertaining this idea."

"It's not ideal, I'll grant you that, but by pretending to be your boyfriend, we have a tactical advantage. It could make all the difference if things go south."

Scott rose from the sofa and crossed the room. He gently cupped Willow's shoulders. "Please, do this for me.

I'm the reason you're in danger. Let me protect you. If I—" His voice cracked. "Losing you would break me."

Logan tore his gaze away from the emotional scene, feeling like an intruder on a private family moment, but not before seeing Willow's hard expression soften. It was clear she and Scott had a special connection. Would Logan ever have such a deep bond with Mia? He wanted to, but didn't know how to get there.

"Okay, Uncle Scott." Willow hugged him and then pulled back. "But I have a few demands of my own. The security detail can accompany me to fundraising and campaign events. However, I don't want them following me around at home or work."

Scott opened his mouth to protest, but this time, it was Logan who interjected. "That's better for me. Willow is most vulnerable when she's at home alone. I'd rather have men I can completely trust keeping guard on the property. I'll talk to my friends."

The older man slowly nodded. "I'll agree to that."

"Good." Willow turned to Logan. "Are you sure about this?"

He met her gaze. The plan was riddled with potential complications, but the threats against Willow were serious. Logan couldn't walk away and leave her unprotected. "Absolutely."

"All right. What happens next?"

FIVE

Willow swiped on tinted lip balm and eyed her reflection in the mirror before tucking an errant strand of her blonde hair behind one ear. Her pencil skirt and heels were professional enough for the office, but perhaps too businesslike for a date. She removed her blazer, revealing the silky straps of her blouse.

Did it look like she was trying too hard? Or not hard enough? It'd been a thousand years since she was last on a date. Uncharacteristic nerves jittered her stomach as she shoved her arms back into the blazer and buttoned it while silently admonishing herself. This wasn't a real date. Logan couldn't care less what she was wearing. It was far too cold to go without the jacket anyway, since mid-October had ushered in a front that dropped the temperatures securely into fall weather.

Squaring her shoulders, she refused another glance in the mirror and stepped out of the bathroom. The hallway of Blessed Hearts Youth Center was bustling with controlled chaos as kids and staff meandered through the rooms.

Several teens were sitting together, heads bent in the library, working on a school project. Another group was gathered in the break room. The drone of Mr. Matthews, math and science tutor extraordinaire, leaked from a classroom. Beyond the large floor-to-ceiling windows, in the grassy backyard, a feisty game of baseball was underway.

All of it brought a smile to Willow's face. She'd worked for five years to build the youth center to what it was today —a bustling hive of energy. Expanding the program by adding an outdoor recreational area would give her teens more ways to connect with each other. Basketball courts, a proper baseball field, swimming pool, and hiking trails. She would even have a gardening area.

But first, she had to raise the funds.

Her cell phone buzzed, and she glanced at her smartwatch to view the texted message. Logan and his family were at the front desk.

Fresh butterflies alighted in her stomach. Willow shoved them down.

Not a real date. You're giving his family a tour of the youth center. Then you and Logan will go to dinner. But it's not a real date.

The mantra replayed in her mind as she crossed the lobby. Logan, handsomely dressed in dark jeans and a polo shirt, turned at the sound of her heels on the tile floor. His dark eyes warmed and a smile touched the corner of his lips. Once again, Willow questioned the wisdom of asking Logan to play her boyfriend for the next two weeks. Already she sensed the danger to her heart. She'd always had a weakness for dark-haired men with broad shoulders. Add in the fact that he'd saved her life last night... well, it was going to be difficult to keep her distance. But she had to. This was a business arrangement. Nothing more.

Conscious of the receptionist watching from the front desk, Willow's steps faltered as she drew closer to Logan. Should she greet him with a handshake? A hug? She decided neither, for the time being, especially since he had his mother and Mia in tow. Instead, Willow forced a bright smile and said, "Hi, Logan." Then she turned to the older woman at his side and extended her hand. "I'm Willow Cassidy. It's lovely to meet you."

"Julia Keller." Her handshake was gentle, but there was a warmth in her eyes that resembled Logan's. Julia smiled and dimples appeared in her cheeks. "Thank you so much for taking the time to give us a tour."

"It's my pleasure." Willow turned to the teen lurking behind both adults. "You must be Mia." She extended her hand toward the young woman, but got an eye roll in response. Her hunched shoulders and negative attitude indicated Mia didn't want to be there but had been coerced into walking over the threshold.

Willow didn't take offense. She'd dealt with more difficult teenagers than Mia and had learned never to take the rejection personally. She knew from experience that it was often a need for control that drove the actions. In her own dark time after losing her parents, she was reckless and obstinate. It was downright embarrassing to remember her poor treatment of others.

"Mia." Logan's tone was sharp. "Don't be rude."

"I'm only here so I can use my cell phone later, like you promised. It's ridiculous that you took it away in the first place. I'm already suffering through detention for skipping class." She crossed her arms over her chest. "Whatever. You don't care. I'm here for the tour, okay? No one said I had to like it."

Color rose in Julia's cheeks, highlighting her embarrassment at the family squabble. Willow cast her a reassuring smile, and when Logan opened his mouth to correct his niece, she cut him off by saying, "Let's start the tour, shall we?"

She led the group through the main areas of the youth center, showing them the facilities and making introductions along the way when appropriate. Mia was quiet and, for the most part, appeared uninterested, but Willow noticed her gaze drifting around a time or two. The music rooms held her interest. Not surprising, given what Logan had shared yesterday about his niece playing the piano. Willow left the small auditorium for the last stop. She paused with her hand on the door. "Please be quiet as we enter. Practice is in progress."

Piano music filtered through the space. Nerves jittered in Willow's stomach. She hoped her calculation would pay off. Sending out a silent prayer, she rounded the corner. Behind her, Mia inhaled sharply. The teenager blinked at the woman sitting on the bench in front of the grand piano.

"No way." Her mouth gaped open. "That's... that's Josie Fuentes."

Logan's brow creased. "Who?"

Mia didn't answer, transfixed by the woman in front of her. Josie was lost in her music, fingers dancing over the keys in graceful precision. Nineteen and youthful, her blonde hair was pulled into a messy bun and she was dressed in a graphic shirt and dark jeans.

Willow leaned over and whispered to Logan, "Josie is a star musician with one of the most popular Christian rock bands, His Guiding Light. When you told me Mia used to play for the church choir, I figured she'd heard of Josie and was a fan."

He blinked, surprise rippling across his handsome features. "You remembered that?"

For a moment, Willow was lost in the depths of his dark brown eyes. The scent of his aftershave tickled her nose. It was masculine but not overpowering. Heat from his body seemed to radiate in her direction. Too close. She was standing too close to him.

Willow pulled back but kept her voice pitched low. "Josie was one of the first teenagers I mentored when the youth center opened. She's estranged from her dad, and her mom had just died. You wouldn't know it to see her now, but Josie was failing school and heading down a dangerous path with the wrong kind of people. I explained to Josie before y'all came that Mia is going through a rough patch. She'll help do the heavy lifting. If Josie talks about how much the youth center helped her, hopefully it'll encourage Mia to try it too."

A final note echoed through the space. Willow clapped, joined by Logan, his mom, and Mia. Josie smiled, although a pretty pink flushed her cheeks. She might've been one of the most sought-after musicians, but she maintained a humble and grateful presence.

Willow stepped forward and made the introductions. Josie and Mia immediately started discussing songs, and within ten minutes, the two of them were bent over a blank piece of sheet music, crafting their own unique creation.

"You've performed a miracle, Willow. Mia is smiling. I haven't seen her this happy or excited in a long time." Logan watched his niece with affection. "Thank you."

"There's no need to thank me. I'm happy to help. Convincing difficult teenagers to go in the right direction is my job, you know."

He chuckled. "You make it look easy." He glanced around the auditorium. "What made you start Blessed Hearts? Teenagers aren't usually the ones people provide resources for. They can be... challenging."

"They can, which is exactly what made me focus on them. I went through a hard time myself while in my teens." Willow took a deep breath. She'd shared about her past with others before, but telling her story never got easier. "My parents died in a plane crash when I was thirteen. Grief and loss sent me on a disastrous path. I was suicidal, even. My uncle, God bless him, was at a complete loss on how to help me. He'd never had children of his own, and while he cared very much, he's a tough-love type. Out of desperation, he sent me to live with my grandmother for a summer. My father's mother. Best thing that ever happened to me. Grandma Jean spent every day talking to me about God's love. Forgiveness. Choosing wisely. She saved my life."

Willow's heart ached. She missed her grandmother dearly. "Grandma Jean passed away shortly after I graduated with my masters, but the lessons she taught me are what I based the center on." Willow gestured toward Josie and Mia across the room, playing the piano together. "Nothing gives me greater joy than seeing the mission in action."

Logan was quiet for a long moment. "What you're doing is very special. I admire it."

"It's a gift given by God. We all have them." She tilted her head and studied him. "You're a paramedic. I'm awed by that. You literally save people's lives on a daily basis."

"And yet it's the ones I don't save that haunt me." The words came out in a whisper, as if Logan hadn't meant to say them. His gaze was lost and distant. "Combat teaches hard lessons. You have to lock down your emotions to get the job done." He lifted his gaze to meet hers. "It's the exact opposite of parenting. I'm more like your uncle in that regard. Tough love is all I know how to give."

"It's still love." Her heart wept at the vulnerability in his expression. This connection between them defied logic. She barely knew Logan, and yet some part of her felt like she'd known him forever. "How many times were you deployed?"

"More than I can count."

"Did you ever get hurt?"

Logan nodded. "During a rescue mission, I was shot three times. Lost a kidney. I was on the final stretch of my recovery when my brother and sister-in-law died. That's when I moved here to take care of Mia. My parents help as much as they can, but they're getting older in years. It's not easy for them either."

He had the weight of the world on his shoulders, caring for a grieving teenager and his aging parents. Willow was touched by Logan's dedication to his family. "Mia's fortunate to have you. I know it's hard, but you're doing the best you can. No one can ask for more than that."

Their gazes met. Once again, Willow became increasingly aware of how close their bodies were. The air crackled with a delicious tension that sparked a riot of butterflies in her stomach. She was powerless to move forward or back. Frozen in place. The rest of the room melted away, leaving her fixed on Logan. Her mind absorbed all the tiny details she hadn't noticed before. The faint ridge along his nose indicating it might have been broken once and the faded scar along the edge of one eyebrow. Her breath stalled in her chest when his attention dropped to her mouth.

Logan cleared his throat. "I don't know about you, but I'm starving. Why don't we head to dinner? I'll let my mom know that we're leaving."

Willow inhaled, the spell between them broke. "I'll let my official bodyguards know. They'll want to follow us to the restaurant."

Those pesky nerves returned and stayed throughout the short drive to the Italian restaurant on Main Street. The waitress showed them to a table for two in the rear with windows overlooking the town square. Children played soccer while parents chatted in small groups. More people meandered from shop to shop. The sunset painted colors of muted purples and oranges across the sky. Willow was so busy admiring the view, it took several seconds for her to realize Logan had pulled out her chair and was waiting for her to sit.

"Oh, thank you." Heat flushed her cheeks and she fumbled with her napkin, knocking a knife off the table. Logan caught the utensil before it hit the floor. She stared up at him in surprise, more heat rising in her face. She wanted to lift the tablecloth and hide under it. "I'm... I'm not normally this clumsy."

"My reflexes aren't normally that fast." He winked, setting the knife back on the table.

She chuckled. Logan had a way of easing her anxiety without calling attention to it. His easygoing nature was extremely attractive. Once again, Willow questioned the wisdom of having Logan pretend to be her boyfriend for the next few weeks. She wasn't interested in a romantic relationship, but sometimes, emotions had a way of clouding judgment. Willow had learned that lesson the hard way.

The best way to handle things was head-on. Discussing the rules and boundaries would make things easier.

The waitress took their drink order and disappeared. Willow's bodyguards were silent sentries. One kept watch on the entrance, the other on the street. A constant reminder of the danger she was in.

"We should discuss how this is going to work." She fiddled with the menu. "It's been years since I've been on a date... not that this is a date. I mean it's a fake date." She shook her head. "This is confusing. When my uncle suggested this arrangement, it seemed like a simple answer to the problem, but the reality is far more complicated. I don't want things to be misconstrued between us."

Logan placed his hand over hers. His touch was warm and comforting. Strength. The man eluded strength by simply breathing. Willow's heart skipped a beat.

"Relax." Logan kept his voice pitched low. "You and I both know the truth. This is an act between us, nothing more. Treat me as you would any man you're interested in." He lifted his lips in a heart-stopping smile. "That includes holding my hand and gazing lovingly into my eyes as this reporter snaps our photograph through the window."

Willow desperately wanted to turn her head but resisted. "The leak from my uncle's office worked." Scott strategically had Logan's name released to the public, along with a general hint that a romance was brewing between them since the rescue. "Point of no return. Are you regretting it yet?"

"Not even a bit. Spending time with a beautiful, smart woman isn't a hardship."

A warmth spread through Willow. Beautiful and smart? Did he really think so?

She cut those thoughts off with a snap. Logan was right. Nothing they said during the next two weeks meant anything. Both of them were playing a role, and she would be wise to keep her emotions in check.

Her cell beeped with an incoming text. Willow shook her head and fumbled for her purse. "Sorry. I meant to turn my phone on silent during dinner, but forgot. I consider it rude for notifications to continuously interrupted the evening."

"That's something we have in common. I took Mia's phone away because she skipped class last week and thought we'd actually talk during mealtime instead of battling over whether she can have her phone at the dinner table." He sighed. "You can imagine just how well that's going. I'm starting to think I'm the one being punished and not her."

Willow chuckled. "Parenting a teen isn't easy. They know just the right way to make life miserable."

"You can say that again."

She pulled out her cell. The text message became visible on the screen and her body went ice cold. The noise of the restaurant faded until all Willow could hear was the pounding of her heart. Her hand gripped the phone with white knuckles. "Logan—"

Her throat closed and she couldn't get out the words. Instead, she turned the cell phone toward him and watched as his expression darkened. A muscle in his jaw worked as he read the message. Then his gaze shot to the window, his eyes searching.

Searching for someone watching them.

Willow dropped her cell on the table, but the message stayed on the screen, glowing like a beacon of hatred.

I failed to kill you last night, but this isn't over. Enjoy dinner with your boyfriend. It may be your last meal. Or it may not. I decide.

Either way, your days are numbered.

SIX

Darkness coated the neighborhood as Logan slipped around the side of Willow's house during a perimeter check. Grass padded his footsteps. The night air was crisp and fragrant with the scents of leaves and damp earth. Moonlight provided just enough illumination for him to see into the generous backyard. Willow lived on two acres about twenty minutes from the youth center. The house was modest, but improvements had been made to the outdoor area. Flowers grew in artful arrangements near a covered patio with an outdoor kitchen complete with a BBQ and pizza oven. Fruit trees—pear, peach, and apple—were scattered throughout the perfect meadow of grass.

A gate in the rear led to a walking path that meandered down to a creek. He checked the padlock, ensuring it was secure. Willow's security system was top-of-the-line and would alert if someone entered the yard, but nothing was foolproof. If someone wanted to get onto the property to kill her, they would find a way. Logan wouldn't let his guard down for a moment.

Especially not after the text she'd received at dinner.

Please, Lord, give me the strength to help her. Guide me to make the best decisions.

The prayer eased some of the burden weighing on his shoulders. He wasn't in this alone. God was a constant and comforting presence.

Logan's phone beeped with an alert from the security system. He'd already connected his phone to the cameras so he could monitor them. Several cars had pulled into the driveway, and through the livestream video, Logan watched as his friends piled out. The cavalry had arrived.

Logan picked up his pace across the yard to the back door. He entered the kitchen. It was spacious, with a large picture window and a butcher-block island. The coffee pot gurgled as it brewed. Pastries and various desserts were plated and sat on the table. Voices filtered from the living room. Logan shrugged off his jacket, tossed it on a peg next to the door, and removed his boots before turning the corner to greet his friends. "Hey, guys."

There was a round of brotherly hugs. Willow stood back, lingering in the foyer. She'd changed from her suit into a set of yoga pants and a soft long-sleeved shirt while Logan was checking the perimeter. A headband pushed her bangs off her face, but a few loose strands had wriggled free to sweep across her forehead. She wasn't wearing makeup. The fresh-faced, relaxed look only emphasized her natural beauty.

Logan went to her side and placed a hand on the small of her back. Without heels, she barely reached his shoulder. An indescribable emotion swept over him. More than attraction, more than a protectiveness. It was an emotional connection that made him want to ease her discomfort. Logan wanted to pass it off as mere kindness, or a friendly gesture, but it was a lie. The spark that ignited on the night he saved Willow's life was slowly growing into something more.

He needed to be careful here. Otherwise, this game of pretend they were playing would end in heartbreak. Logan didn't have room in his life for a romantic relationship. He was barely treading water as it was.

"Willow, I'd like you to meet my friends." He pointed to each man in turn. "Jason Gonzalez is a former Marine and that's his dog, Connor. Nathan Hollister is a former Green Beret. He runs a horse rescue with his wife, Cassie. His cousin, Kyle Stewart, is a security specialist. Tucker Colburn is a former Army Ranger who works for the Knoxville Police Department. And that's Walker Montgomery. He was a Navy SEAL." Logan glanced down at Willow. "That was a lot of information all at once, but over the next couple of days, you'll get to know them."

"And our significant others." Kyle grinned. "The minute I told my wife that Logan's girlfriend was in danger, Sierra started making plans with the other ladies to help. They're ready to adopt you into the fold."

"Uhhh." Logan struggled to find the right words. Several of his friends had fallen in love while protecting someone. It wasn't strange to them, or their significant others, that Logan started dating Willow after saving her life or that their relationship was developing at warp speed. But there was one giant difference in this case.

Logan and Willow were faking it.

He didn't like lying to his friends, but telling them the

truth wasn't possible at the moment. None of his buddies would reveal the secret on purpose, but there was always a chance someone would accidentally slip. Gossip spread like wildfire in Knoxville. It was too great a risk. He planned to come clean once the case was over and prayed they would understand. "I appreciate the sentiment, guys, but it might be better—"

"Save it." Nathan held up a hand. "There's no talking the ladies out of something once their mind is made up."

The married men among the group laughed. Tucker, still wearing his police uniform, gently shoved Logan's shoulder. "This dude never dates. We were sure he'd stay single forever." Tucker grinned at Willow. "You may regret taking him on. He's messy, has the worst table manners, and secretly loves reality television shows."

Willow's mouth flattened, as if she was holding back a laugh. "And I was afraid it would be hard to get the dirt on Logan from his friends."

"Nope. We'll tell you whatever you want to know."

Logan shoved Tucker good-naturedly. The teasing was all in good fun. "Cut it out. Get in the kitchen before I kick your rear end."

"I'd like to see you try," Tucker shot back. "And watch who you're pushing around. Threatening a police officer is a crime."

The ribbing continued as they piled into the kitchen. The next few minutes were spent pouring coffee and selecting desserts. Logan nearly laughed at the way Willow's eyebrows rose when she saw how quickly the sweets disappeared. He leaned over and whispered in her ear, "They like to eat."

She chuckled. "I see that."

Once everyone was settled, Logan ran through everything they knew so far. The men were stone faced by the time he was finished. They joked with each other and wrestled like juveniles, but when it came to safeguarding innocents, each of his friends took the task seriously. Logan was relieved to have their involvement. He couldn't protect Willow alone, and relying on unknown bodyguards wasn't good enough. He needed men he could trust on his team.

And he trusted these guys. With his life. And with Willow's.

Jason rubbed the scar on the left side of his face before reaching down to pat the German shepherd stationed at his side. Connor licked his owner's hand. The two of them were inseparable, having worked in war zones together before returning stateside with injuries that ended their careers. "Was Chief Garcia able to trace the cell phone the text message was sent from?"

"Burner phone, as expected." Logan asked Willow for her cell, opened it to the message, and set it on the table. "Whoever sent this text wanted to make it clear the attack on her wasn't random. He wants to terrorize her."

"It's working." Willow gripped her coffee mug with both hands, as if trying to absorb warmth from the porcelain. "My family has received death threats before, but nothing like this. They've always been sent to publicly known addresses, like business emails and such. Never to my personal cell phone."

Jason frowned. "Do you have a separate cell phone for your business?"

"No. I like having personal contact with my staff. It's never been an issue before today."

"Understandable, but it doesn't narrow things down. Considering how many people have your number, it wouldn't be difficult for the attacker to get his hands on it." Jason turned to Tucker. "Where is the investigation regarding the bodyguard?"

"Chief Garcia has confirmed there was a payoff." Tucker leaned back in his chair. Light played off the police badge pinned to his chest. "Bruce Snyder received a large sum of money a few days before the attack on Willow. There were direct messages between him and an unknown party, which explained the plan. Bruce would create an opening for the attacker to nab Willow. Something went awry, though, because the bodyguard was shot."

"Or the killer was tying up a loose end," Kyle pointed out.

Tucker nodded. "Possibly. Although it's hard to reason why he would go to all the trouble to pay the man only to kill him. Either way, it doesn't really matter. The end result is the same." He grabbed a brownie from the plate in the center. "Are we sure these threats are connected to Scott's senate campaign? Chief Garcia and I are running down the names Scott provided to us of criminals he's put away and so far we're coming up empty-handed."

"Nothing is certain, but it seems like the most likely scenario." Logan reached for a file folder on the table and opened it. He spread copies of the stalking photographs taken of Willow across the surface. "Before the attack at the youth center, these pictures were sent to her uncle's campaign office. Someone's been stalking her."

Walker reached for the papers and flipped through them, a frown darkening his face. The former Navy SEAL had no tolerance for women being threatened or hurt. His own sister had been killed over a decade ago and the tragic loss was still something he wrestled with. He got to the last one and laid the pages back down. "These were designed to scare Scott. Why? What does the perpetrator want? There's no message accompanying the photographs."

"Revenge." Willow gripped her coffee mug. "My uncle worked as a federal prosecutor for over thirty years. He put a lot of dangerous criminals behind bars. His recent senate campaign has put him in the spotlight."

Walker was quiet for a long moment. Logan could practically see the wheels in his friend's head turning. "What are you thinking?"

"It doesn't strike me as a revenge move. If someone wanted to kill Willow to get back at Scott, why warn him it was going to happen? He has the means and ability to put a full security detail around her." Walker gestured to the pictures. "By sending these, the attacker tipped his hand."

"The same thought occurred to me." Logan pushed his plate aside. "If we assume these photographs are connected to the attacks against Willow—and it seems likely they are given the timing—then the killer is sending a message to Scott."

Walker nodded. "I could be way off base here, but the incumbent senator—the one Scott is running against—has a shady reputation. Two years ago, the Austin Police Department investigated him for the assault of a local contractor when the man complained about an illegal bidding process. Senator Randall was cleared ultimately, but it's not the first time he's been accused of tipping the scales in his favor. Right now, he's trailing in the polls..."

His friend had voiced the worries plaguing Logan over the last few hours. Senator Jerry Randall had a reputation of playing dirty. Scandal had followed him for his entire career, everything from tax fraud to hiring hitmen. So far, none of the accusations had resulted in an arrest, but it was hard to ignore how his problems seemed to melt away. Newspaper reporters stopped investigating things, witnesses were silenced and so forth. The man came from a wealthy and influential family. He could be using his connections and his money to silence people. Senator Randall wouldn't be the first politician to do so.

Beside him, Willow inhaled sharply. "Are you suggesting Senator Randall is attempting to kill me so my uncle will drop out of the campaign?" She reared back, horrified. "That's preposterous."

"Is it?" Logan placed a hand over hers and gave it a reassuring squeeze. Her skin was soft, the ridges of her knuckles delicate. "I'm not one to believe random rumors, but numerous people have accused Senator Randall of shady or illegal dealings. In the last election, his opponent dropped out under the guise of an illness, but there were rumblings his family had been threatened. If that's true and Senator Randall was behind the threats, then what's stopping him from doing it again?"

Willow frowned. "I know Senator Randall walks very close to the line of legality and he doesn't serve in his constituents' best interest. It's one of the big reasons my uncle entered the senatorial race. But murder? Threats?

That's a huge accusation and we have no evidence of his involvement."

"True, but right now, we need to keep an open mind."

"But wouldn't it make more sense to kill my uncle? He's the candidate."

"It's also more obvious. By threatening you, Senator Randall can accomplish the same goal with some level of deniability." Logan let Willow absorb his counter argument and then continued, "Chief Garcia is focused on tracking down the criminals your uncle put away. He doesn't have the manpower nor does he have the ability—for political reasons—to investigate Senator Randall. We can."

She pulled her hand away from him, her gaze jumping from person to person. "No. Absolutely not. If Senator Randall finds out we're investigating him, it could ruin my uncle's campaign."

"We'll be discreet." Jason's voice was laced with confidence. "It's not the first time we've looked into a high-profile person. In fact, I wouldn't be surprised if that's why Chief Garcia recommended us to your uncle in the first place."

Tucker nodded. "He hasn't said anything to me, but the chief is smart. He knows we'd eventually head in this direction."

Logan turned toward Willow. "Last year, we investigated Oliver Patterson. Like Senator Randall, the police believed Oliver was engaged in criminal activity, but couldn't prove it. We helped uncover the truth."

Oliver had threatened his own flesh and blood, his daughter Sierra and his grandson, Daniel. They were thrust into a dangerous situation, but it all worked out in the end. Now Sierra was married to Tucker. The former Army

Ranger had transitioned to family life with ease. He was a wonderful father to Daniel and was talking about having more kids.

"I remember reading about that case in the news." Willow studied the grain on the table for several heartbeats. She finally sighed. "I want to discuss the matter with my uncle before we do anything about Senator Randall. We can speak to Uncle Scott tomorrow after the car wash fundraiser."

Logan didn't like the delay, but he understood her hesitation. "Okay, we'll table that for tomorrow."

Willow nodded, but worry clouded her eyes. Logan didn't take it personally. They were asking for a lot of trust and faith from her. She wasn't exaggerating the risk to her uncle. If word of their clandestine investigation became public knowledge, it would create a media scandal for Scott and potentially cost him the election. Logan and his team would make sure that wouldn't happen.

Kyle gathered the photos on the table. "Forward me the emails that were sent to your uncle's campaign. I'll try to trace their origin."

"Kyle is a security specialist." Logan explained to Willow. Kyle was actually a military-trained hacker, but very few people knew the ins and outs of his career. Not even Logan knew it all. Sometimes working for Uncle Sam meant carrying certain secrets to your grave. "If anyone can trace the message, it's Kyle. You can trust him."

Willow nodded. "Of course. Do whatever you need to." She smiled at the men surrounding her table. "I see why Chief Garcia calls you guys the Special Forces. No wonder he recommended you. I feel safer already."

They made a plan to protect Willow over the next few days and then the guys said their goodbyes.

Logan lingered, helping Willow clean up the dishes. When she stifled a yawn, he took it as a sign he needed to go. She walked him to the front door. "Thank you for listening to my concerns about investigating Senator Randall. It may seem silly, but I don't want to do anything that might jeopardize my uncle's chance of winning without speaking to him first."

"It's not silly, it's respectful. I completely understand." Logan removed his jacket from the hook by the door and shrugged it on. "Jason and Kyle will keep watch over your house tonight; then Walker and Tucker will take over tomorrow. They're trained soldiers, so you won't see them, but rest assured they'll be there."

His cell phone vibrated. Logan removed it from his pocket, glancing at the caller ID. Concern ricocheted through him. "Hi, Chief Garcia. Everything okay?"

"No. Are you with Willow, by any chance?"

Logan met her questioning glance. "I am. Why?"

"You both need to come down to the station." Chief Garcia's tone was grave. "I've got your niece here with me. I'm sorry, Logan, but I had to arrest her."

SEVEN

The next day, Willow sat behind her desk at the youth center. Exhaustion tugged at her muscles, the result of a restless night's sleep followed by a hectic Saturday morning running a car wash fundraising event. Music from the parking lot filtered through the closed window accompanied by the sounds of laughter from the teens still sudsing the last of the vehicles. The fundraiser had gone off without a hitch. That fact brought Willow a lot of joy, but it was tempered by the threats against her life and the task in front of her now.

Across the wide expanse of the desk, Mia was hunched in the visitor's chair closest to the door. She wore combat boots, dark jeans with a hole in the right knee, and a flannel shirt. The ever-present scowl was etched on her face, but there was a hint of embarrassment in the crease of her brows and the constant way she twisted a strand of hair through her fingers. She also refused to meet Willow's eyes. Not surprising since the teen had been arrested while attempting to break into the youth center.

Logan loomed over Mia. His expression was rigid, his jaw clenched so tightly it was any wonder he didn't crack his molars. Underneath the anger, Willow sensed his fear and frustration. Along with his humiliation. Last night had been a long, trying ordeal and this meeting wouldn't go any better if he didn't calm down.

"Logan, take a seat." Willow gestured to the other visitor's chair. "Please."

He spared her a glance, and she arched her brows ever so slightly to indicate her disapproval. Any other man probably would've missed the gesture, but Logan was far from ordinary. His mouth pursed, but then he marched to the chair and sat stiffly.

Willow focused back on Mia. "I asked your uncle to bring you here this morning because there are some decisions that need to be made. You were arrested for breaking and entering the youth center. Chief Garcia has asked if I want to press charges. The punishment if the case goes forward could include juvenile detention. Do you understand?"

Mia's complexion paled. She nodded.

"Good. Before I make my decision, I want to hear your side of things." She held the young woman's gaze. "And I expect the truth. If you aren't willing to tell the truth, then please get up and leave my office immediately."

She shifted uncomfortably in the chair before licking her lips. "I'm sorry. I shouldn't have broken into the center. It was a dumb thing to do."

"I won't argue with that, but I'd like to know why you did it."

Two spots of color appeared on Mia's cheeks. Again,

she shifted in her chair. "My friend Debbie dared me to. She promised to buy me a new cell phone if I stole something of Josie's." Her jaw tightened, and for a moment, she looked so similar to Logan, it was hard to believe she wasn't his child. "My uncle took away my cell last week, and it's absolutely humiliating. I'm the only kid in my school without one."

"I took it away because you skipped class," Logan bit out. "Which is unacceptable. As is breaking into the youth center."

Mia glared at him. "You're not my dad. Stop trying to be."

The arrow she threw hit its mark, judging from the way Logan's body stiffened. A myriad of emotions flickered across his features before he tucked them away. His voice was steady when he spoke next. "No, I'm not your dad, but I am someone who cares about you. You're better than this."

The anger melted from Mia's expression as she sagged against the visitor's chair. Her gaze dropped to the carpeting, and she fingered a lock of her hair again. Her chin trembled. All at once, Willow could see the little girl hiding inside the hardened teenage shell. It was clear Mia was in pain. Lost and floating on a sea of uncertainty. Willow's heart broke for her. She'd been there and remembered exactly how lonely it felt.

Logan's expression was placid, but grief vibrated off him. Mia wasn't the only one struggling. He'd lost a brother and sister-in-law, then became a single parent overnight to a hurting teenager. It touched something deep inside Willow. Once again, she was struck at the similarity between Logan and her own uncle. Both of them were strong men who did everything possible for their family.

Mia blinked rapidly and swiped at her eyes. "Are you going to press charges, Ms. Cassidy?"

"That depends on you. I'm willing to tell Chief Garcia to drop all charges, but only if you agree to my conditions."

Suspicion creased Mia's features. "Which are?"

"Every day after school for the next month, you'll come straight to the center. You will attend one hour of counseling and one hour of tutoring to get your grades up. I also expect you to pay for the window that you broke by working at the center doing various odd jobs."

Mia was quiet for a long moment. "And if I do all these things, you promise to drop the charges?"

"You have my word." Willow rose from her chair and circled her desk until she was standing in front of Mia. Then she extended her hand. "Do we have a deal?"

Mia hesitated. Then she stood and shook Willow's hand. "We have a deal."

"Good. You can start today by helping with the cleanup from the car wash event. Ms. Jackson is supervising." Willow's deputy director was an organizational ninja and kept the entire center running like clockwork. "Let her know you're volunteering and she'll give you a job."

Mia nodded and moved toward the door. Before she could leave, Willow called out her name. "One more thing. Josie is practicing in the auditorium. I'd like you to stop by and apologize to her."

For a second, Willow thought Mia was about to refuse, but then she swallowed the reply and simply nodded. Fresh embarrassment heated her cheeks. Apologizing to Josie wouldn't be easy, but it was the right thing to do. And Mia knew it.

She left, gently shutting the door behind her.

Logan leaned forward, propped his elbows on his knees, and pitched his head between his hands. Willow gently cupped his shoulder. The fabric of his button-down shirt was warm to the touch, the muscles under her palm firm. She didn't bother asking if he was okay. He wasn't.

After a moment, he raised his head and took a long, deep breath. "Sorry. I'm..." He ran a hand over his face. "This is a mess. I'm screwing this up. I have no idea what my brother was thinking when he made me Mia's guardian."

"He knew you would love her." Willow's heart ached to hear the pain in his voice. None of this was easy, and he was being far too hard on himself. "I know you're worried, Logan, but she made good decisions in this room today, and that's an excellent first step in the right direction. Let's pray she continues on this path."

He nodded. "You're right." Logan rose, taking her hands into his. "Thank you, Willow. I'm supposed to be the one protecting you, not bringing more trouble to your doorstep."

Willow met his gaze and her breath caught. Logan's eyes were a rich brown deepened by flecks the color of cocoa. She felt lost in their midst. With one more step, she'd be within the circle of his arms, one slight movement and their lips would meet. Desire flared in her belly. Before she could fully stop herself, Willow's body tilted forward. It took every ounce of will to halt the momentum. Her mind wrestled with a tangle of thoughts.

Mike betrayed her. That hurt wasn't something she'd

fully recovered from. Logan wasn't her ex—that was obvious —but the arrangement between them was professional. A business contract. Developing romantic feelings for each other wasn't part of the bargain. And it was too much of a risk. She needed Logan's protection.

Willow squeezed his hands and forced herself to take a step back. "You don't need to thank me, Logan. You saved my life. Helping Mia is the least I can do." She moved toward the door. "Come on. I should get back to the car wash."

The lobby doors of the youth center were flung wide open, teens bustling back and forth with various supplies. Warm sunshine took the edge off the November chill. Country music played from a set of speakers set up near the tree line. Soap bubbles and water streaked across the asphalt.

Jason, along with his dog Connor, were standing at the edge of the parking lot, speaking to a customer having his vehicle washed. Tucker was also on duty, chatting with a couple of the teens. He looked relaxed, but his gaze never settled in one place. Having their presence at the car wash was a relief. Willow trusted them—along with Logan—to keep the event safe.

Susan Jackson, the youth center's deputy director, made a beeline for Willow. Her dyed brown hair was pulled into a high ponytail, and her eyes twinkled with excitement. "The event was a huge success. We're one-fourth of the way toward our goal so far."

"That's fantastic." They'd been running fundraising events for the last week, plus additional donations had been made through their website. It was a relief to know it was having an impact. Willow desperately wanted to see the outdoor recreation area built. "Please update the sign in the lobby. It's going to mean a lot to the kids to see how far we've come."

"Will do." She patted Willow's arm before heading inside, her ponytail swinging with the force of her steps. Susan was a bundle of energy. She rarely stayed in one place for too long.

Logan rocked back on his heels. "I saw the design for the outdoor recreational center in the lobby. It's an ambitious project." He gestured to the woods extending behind the west side of the parking lot. "You're putting it over there, right? I didn't realize before seeing the layout that Blessed Hearts owned all of that property."

"When I started the youth center, I bought the building and fifteen additional acres for future expansion using the inheritance from my parents. There was enough money left over to create a trust. That's how Blessed Hearts pays for its operating expenses every year, and will for decades to come, but we need to fundraise for any additional projects."

Logan's brow furrowed. "Sorry, you lost me on the trust part. How does it pay for your expenses?"

Willow wasn't surprised by the question. It came up quite a bit. "Basically, I took my inheritance and invested in a very safe way. That money generates income, much like a rental house does for a landlord."

"Oh, so as long as you have the rental house, it'll continue to bring in income. Smart."

She nodded. "Exactly. This way Blessed Hearts doesn't have to worry about constantly fundraising to pay staff or our light bill. But if we want to expand our program, like with the outdoor recreational center, we have to ask for donations." A light breeze ruffled her bangs. Willow shoved the longer stands behind her ear. "The teens have been asking for more outdoor activities since the youth center opened. We built a makeshift baseball field, but it's going to be amazing to provide additional facilities. The counselors are especially excited about the hiking trails and the gardening areas."

"It sounds wonderful." Logan's gaze drifted across the parking lot to his niece. She was helping a couple of other teens to wash a truck. "I should've brought Mia here earlier. I'm used to handling personal things on my own." He gave Willow a wry smile. "A side-effect after so many years in the military."

"You aren't the only one. It looks like I have everything figured out, but it's not true." Willow was confident when it came to her work, but her personal life was almost nonexistent. It was lonely at times. She had her uncle and a few friends from college, but letting someone in on a deeper level was a struggle.

This wasn't the way she'd envisioned her life at thirty. Marriage. Children. They'd always been part of the plan. Willow was a romantic deep down, but opening herself up again to love was scary after her ex's betrayal.

Why was she even thinking about this right now?

Logan. Logan was the reason why. Spending time with him—even under these dangerous circumstances—was raising questions in her mind. Issues she'd long since put to rest were rearing to the surface. Willow didn't like it.

"Is that Senator Randall?" Logan asked.

His question jerked Willow's attention back to the

parking lot. An SUV with darkly tinted windows had pulled into an empty space far away from the teens engaging in a soapy water fight now that the car wash was officially over. The sounds of their screams and laughter carried on the breeze.

Willow barely heard it. Her focus locked on Senator Randall as he strolled in her direction. "What is he doing here?"

The question came out in a whisper, low enough for Logan's ears only. He didn't answer. There wasn't time.

Senator Randall reached them. Mid-fifties and fit, he had the healthy vitality of a man who spent his time outdoors playing tennis. His olive complexion contrasted well with his thick crown of salt-and-pepper hair. He was fond of tailored blue suits and designer shoes, which he paired with a variety of colored bow ties. The outfit gave off the appearance of intelligence and trustworthiness. A calculated move, one designed to make Randall resemble a college professor. Or the dean of a prestigious university.

Today, his bowtie was blood red.

"Ms. Cassidy, hello." Senator Randall gave her a charming smile. "I was in the neighborhood doing another event when I heard about the car wash. I couldn't resist coming by to give my support."

The statement caught her off-guard. Willow shook the senator's hand on autopilot as her mind raced. Although she'd met Senator Randall several times at different campaign events, they'd barely exchanged more than a dozen words. He'd never once shown interest in her youth center. Uneasiness swirled in her stomach.

Was she staring into the face of the man who was trying to kill her?

He didn't look like a murderer. Once again, Willow found herself second-guessing the assertions made last night about the senator's involvement in the attack against her. There were far easier ways to win an election.

Another man exited the SUV and quickly snapped a photograph with his cell phone. Willow recognized him as Martin Goodson, the senator's campaign manager. A flash of anger burst through her as the reason for this impromptu visit instantly became clear. Randall was going to use it to promote his campaign. Willow could practically see the headline now: SENATOR SUPPORTS THE NIECE OF OPPOSING CANDIDATE.

She dropped his hand before another photo could be taken. "I'm sorry, Senator, but you're late. The event is over."

If he noticed her curt tone, it didn't faze him. Senator Randall pressed a hand against his bowtie, flattening the edges down. "Never mind. I don't need the car cleaned. I simply want to support the cause, especially given the trouble you've had lately. I read about the attack on you the other night. Horrible." He met her gaze. "Have the police caught the culprit yet?"

"No, although they're working hard on the case. I'm sure they'll find the man responsible."

"Of course they will." Senator Randall shifted his attention to Logan. "You're the young man that saved Willow, aren't you? Logan, am I right? Your photograph was in the paper."

"Yes, sir." Logan hesitated and then shook the senator's hand.

Senator Randall's smile was warm. "Good work." He dropped Logan's hand and turned his attention back to Willow. "Ms. Cassidy, could we talk for a moment in private?"

Without waiting for an answer, he walked a short distance away. Willow glanced at Logan and raised her brows slightly before following the senator. She could feel Logan's gaze on her back. He wouldn't follow, but he also wouldn't let her out of his eyesight.

Senator Randall glanced around to make sure no one could overhear their conversation and then focused on Willow. "We don't know each other well, but I'm very concerned about the threats that've been made against you. The photographs sent to Scott's campaign, the physical attack, and now a text message. Someone has targeted you for a specific reason."

Shock rendered Willow speechless for a moment. "How do you know about the photographs and the text message?"

"This is my district, Ms. Cassidy. I always take an interest in any high-profile criminal cases. You'd be surprised how many constituents ask about them."

Was that true? Or did the senator know about the photographs and the text message because he was behind them? Willow didn't know. Her uneasiness grew. She'd assumed the purpose for this visit was a campaign stunt, but now... now she was wondering if there was something far more sinister about it.

Senator Randall held her gaze. "You shouldn't take these threats lightly. Nor should your uncle." His expression took on a sympathetic twist that didn't come across as sincere. "I'd like to say these kinds of threats are unusual, but they aren't. A life in public service comes with risk. It may not be the right avenue for your family and now would be a good time to decide."

Something lurked in the depths of his eyes. Something menacing. It sent a chill down Willow's spine. Suddenly, she could see him as a cold-blooded killer.

She forced herself to hold his gaze. "Thank you for the warning, Senator, but our family has already decided. My uncle won't drop out of the race. Not for any reason."

Martin pulled the phone away from his ear, called the senator's name, and pointed at his watch. Senator Randall nodded in reply before focusing back on Willow. "You'll have to excuse me. Duty calls. It was lovely to see you, Ms. Cassidy. A donation will be made to the youth center through the website. Take care."

With those parting words, the senator turned and crossed the parking lot.

Logan appeared at her side. "What happened?"

"I'm not sure." Willow watched the senator's vehicle pull out of the parking lot. She summarized the conversation. "That was either a campaign stunt or a veiled threat."

Logan's mouth flattened into a thin line. "Maybe it was both."

EIGHT

The Buchanan campaign office was a bustle of activity. The trill of phones ringing collided with the din of conversation as volunteers and staff handled constituent issues. A large whiteboard along one wall contained a map of the district. Logan followed Willow through the open office space filled with desks to a set of stairs leading to the glass-walled offices above. The impromptu visit from Senator Randall didn't sit well with him. The sooner his team could begin investigating, the better.

At the top of the stairs, an elegant woman intercepted them. Logan immediately recognized her from photographs online. Kathryn Buchanan, Scott's wife and Willow's aunt. She was also the campaign manager. Kathryn was dressed in an all-black suit and heels. A strand of pearls decorated her neck. Early forties, she retained the stunning beauty of her news anchor days. A collection of file folders was tucked in the crook of her arm and she carried a cell phone.

"Willow." Kathryn air-kissed her niece's cheeks. "What a surprise. I didn't know you were dropping by this afternoon." Her gaze drifted to Logan. She did an assessing sweep from his shoes to the crown of his head. Kathryn's nose wrinkled slightly in disapproval before she plastered on a courteous smile. "You must be Logan. It's so nice to finally meet you. I couldn't believe it when Scott told me about the attack on Willow. I shudder to think of what might've happened if you hadn't intervened."

She shifted the files in her arm and extended her hand. The nails were manicured and fake.

Logan shook Kathryn's hand. "I was in the right place at the right time."

"Evidently." She released his hand. Her expression was polite and her words pleasant, but there was an iciness to her tone that caught Logan's attention. He couldn't put his finger on it, but he sensed Kathryn did not approve of him. Was it snobbishness? Or something else?

"We need to speak to Uncle Scott," Willow said.

"That's unfortunate." Kathryn gripped the cell phone tight enough to whiten her knuckles as she checked the time. "I've told you time and time again, Willow, you need to call first and set a meeting. Scott's schedule is tight. In fact, we're about to head out for a town hall on the other side of the district."

Willow angled her head to see beyond Kathryn to the office on the right. Scott was encased in the glass walls, seated at a cherry-colored desk, speaking on his cell phone. "It's important. We won't keep him long."

Without waiting for her aunt's reply, Willow stepped around the other woman and headed for her uncle's office. Kathryn's mouth flattened and annoyance flared her nostrils. The glare she shot at Willow's back could have melted the skin off a person. It was obvious there was tension between the two women.

Logan hurried to catch up with Willow. She caught her uncle's eye through the glass, and he waved, holding up a finger to indicate she should wait a moment. She nodded in reply.

Aware they'd caught the attention of some staff members on the lower floor, Logan placed an arm around Willow's waist. The intoxicating scent of her lavender shampoo teased his senses. He pulled her closer, his heart skipping a beat. "There are eyes on us."

She grinned, placing a hand on his chest. That increased his pulse even more. Could she feel his heart racing under her palm? As much as Logan wanted to deny it, being close to Willow was unsettling in an electrifying way. The woman was stunning, but more than that, she was smart and kindhearted. It was incredibly attractive.

"You're a very attentive boyfriend." Willow tilted her head to gaze into his face. The colors in her blue eyes were mesmerizing. Flecks of icy white and deeper blue. There was even a hint of green. "Word is going to get around. If you aren't careful, when we break up, you're going to have women throwing themselves at you."

He snorted. "The last thing on my mind is dating. Mia's keeping me on my toes as it is." Logan kept his voice pitched low to prevent anyone from overhearing their conversation. "Was it my imagination or is there tension between you and Kathryn?"

"That wasn't your imagination." Willow played with a button on his shirt. "Kathryn married my uncle when I was eighteen. We're cordial with each other for his sake, but there's not a lot of affection between us."

"Any particular reason why?"

She shrugged. "Initially, I thought it was simply that we're different types of people. She's an extrovert and very particular about having things done a certain way. Her nails and hair are always perfect. She likes fancy dinner parties, vapid conversation, and champagne." Willow's gaze grew distant. "I'm an introvert. My favorite kind of day is a quiet hike to the lake. I pour my money into the youth center, and while I don't mind dressing up now and then, I couldn't care less about breaking a nail as long as I'm having fun."

Logan sensed Willow had more to say, so he remained quiet.

She sighed. "Despite our differences, I admire Kathryn. She's smart and ambitious. When she and Scott started dating, I was open to the idea. But after they got married, things shifted. I get the feeling Kathryn is jealous of the close relationship I have with Scott. I think she'd prefer him all to herself."

"That's tough." Logan was pained by the thread of hurt vibrating through Willow's voice. How could Kathryn reject her? She was a warm and loving person. "If it's any consolation, Kathryn's the one missing out. Anyone would be fortunate to have you as a member of their family."

Willow's gaze met his and her eyes warmed. "That's incredibly sweet of you to say." She glanced over her shoulder. Kathryn was inside another glass office, having a heated conversation with a red-headed man. "I've made my peace with it. Like I said, we're polite for Uncle Scott's sake. He loves Kathryn deeply, and she makes him happy. That's enough for me."

It was a mature attitude to have. Logan's esteem for Willow was growing in leaps and bounds. Every time she faced a difficult decision, she approached it with consideration and care. It was admirable.

Scott hung up his cell phone and waved them into the office. His dark hair was mussed as if he'd been running his hands through it and his tie was askew. Two different mugs of coffee sat at his elbow. He grabbed one, took a swig, and grimaced.

Willow circled the desk and took the mug from his hand. "Would you like a fresh cup?" She gave him a calculating look. "Or better yet, some water? If you only drink coffee, you won't have a stomach left."

He chuckled, standing to embrace her. "Thank goodness you didn't come to work for the campaign. Otherwise, I'd be on a tofu salads and protein shake diet." Scott pulled back. "I'll get the water. You and Logan sit. Tell me what's on your mind."

"It's about the threats, sir." Logan took a seat on one of the wingback chairs in front of the desk. He quickly explained about the text message Willow received and the unexpected visit from Senator Randall. "All things considered, we should take a hard look at the senator and his potential involvement. He has a reputation for shady dealings. It's possible he's hoping to scare you enough into dropping out of the race by threatening Willow's life."

Scott drummed his fingers on the desk. "Randall is a sneaky weasel. I'm sure his visit today was a campaign stunt. I'm not fond of the man, but I have a hard time imagining he'd threaten my family."

It wasn't an unfair assessment. Logan didn't have any hard evidence, just a gut feeling. He'd learned long ago to honor that intuition. "Randall is smart. He's tangled with law enforcement before and knows how to cover his tracks. Honestly, I doubt he's doing his own dirty work. He's the kind to hire someone to attack Willow. Chief Garcia can't investigate the senator as a potential suspect without hard evidence. I can." Logan kept his tone professional. "It would be foolish to ignore the possibility. Randall has the most to gain if you drop out of the race."

Scott pushed away from the desk and went to the window. He was quiet for a long moment. Willow opened her mouth to speak, but Logan placed a hand on her knee. He sensed her uncle was mulling things over and needed a moment to assess the situation.

"Do it." Scott turned to face them. His tone was clipped and his expression stony. "But don't stop with Jerry Randall. You need to look at his donors and anyone else who has a strong reason to keep him in office."

Willow leaned forward. "Uncle Scott, there's a risk associated with this decision. If the media finds out Logan or his team is digging into Senator Randall, it could blow up your campaign."

"I'm well aware of that." He leveled a pointed look in Logan's direction. "I will do anything to protect my niece. Anything. But winning this election is important to the constituents I'm trying to represent. Senator Randall hasn't done a thing for this district except line his own pockets. It can't continue. If word about your investigation gets out,

I'll deny any knowledge of it. Do we have an understanding?"

"We do." Logan appreciated the older man's directness.

"Good. Keep me advised on what you uncover."

A knock came on the door. Kathryn poked her head in. "We need to go, dear, otherwise we'll be late."

Scott nodded and grabbed his suit jacket from a coat rack. He shrugged it on. Logan shook Scott's hand and stepped back so he could say goodbye to his niece.

Willow straightened Scott's tie. "There are salads on the volunteer snack table downstairs. Grab one on your way out."

"How do you know I haven't already eaten?"

She kissed his cheek. "Because some things never change. Good luck at the town hall."

"Thank you, hon." He started for the door, then snapped his fingers. Scott turned. "The mechanic called an hour ago and said your SUV is ready to be picked up. I'll have someone deliver it to your house tonight."

"Nonsense. We can pick it up on our way back to the youth center." Willow glanced at Logan. "Right?"

"Absolutely."

Scott looked like he was about to argue, but Kathryn tapped her foot and pointed at her watch before exiting the office. He hurried after his wife, catching up to her on the stairs. Logan and Willow followed at a slower pace.

They stepped out into the late-afternoon sunshine and headed for his Jeep. He kept his attention on their surroundings. It would be dangerous to let down his guard after the text message Willow received last night.

The drive to the car mechanic took twenty minutes. No

one followed them. Logan waited while Willow paid for the repairs to her SUV. The attacker had broken her window in an attempt to grab her and rain water had damaged the interior. The memory of that night tugged at Logan. Willow had made an observation to Chief Garcia. Her attacker had a gun and wasn't afraid to use it. He shot the bodyguard. Why hadn't he killed her?

The inconsistency rolled around in his mind as Willow hit a button on her fob. Lights on her SUV blinked and then the engine started.

A wave of heat whooshed over Logan. Muscle memory from decades in the military took over as his body figured out what his mind hadn't registered. He grabbed Willow. His hand cupped the back of her head as they tumbled to the ground. Pain shot through his elbow as they collided with the asphalt. Logan covered Willow's body with his own as parts of her SUV fell all around them. The vehicle was a pile of twisted metal and burning flames. Someone inside the mechanic's shop was screaming.

A bomb. Someone had planted a bomb in her car.

Another explosion rocked the ground as a fresh wave of heat burst from the SUV. More debris rained down.

Willow cried out.

NINE

Willow's hands couldn't stop shaking. She held an ice pack to her forearm where a piece of debris had struck and burned her skin. The Knoxville Police Department was unusually quiet. Most of the deputies were on patrol or running down leads on the latest attack. Rain beat against the glass window of the conference room. The storm raging outside matched the emotional turmoil inside her.

Someone had tried to kill her. Again.

A cup of coffee, a water, and some pretzels sat untouched on the conference table in front of her. Willow couldn't think of eating. She adjusted her hold on the ice pack as Logan strolled into the room. He'd scrubbed the ash and dirt from his face and forearms, but a long scratch raked across the skin at his elbow. His jeans were dusty, his shirt torn at the sleeve, but he was alive. For the second time in days, Logan had saved her life.

What if he'd been hurt? Killed? Unbidden tears flooded her eyes.

Concern creased Logan's features as he crossed the

room to her side in three strides. He knelt down, gently took the ice pack from her arm, and examined the wound. His touch was gentle. "It's hurting more than you thought, isn't it? We can go to the hospital—"

"No, it's not my arm." She drew in a shaky breath, blinking her tears away. "It's everything. Someone could've been seriously hurt today. It's a miracle no one was."

"I know." Logan pulled a chair closer, sat, and then took her hands. "Would it help to pray?"

She nodded, touched that he would offer. Willow squeezed his hands gently and then bowed her head.

"Heavenly Father, we come to you with grateful hearts." Logan's voice was low but thick with emotion. "Thank you for protecting us from danger. Continue to guide our movements and safeguard those around us. In Your name we pray. Amen."

"Amen," Willow echoed. The prayer soothed the rough edges of her frayed emotions. "Thank you, Logan. That was exactly what I needed."

The door to the conference room opened. Chief Garcia marched in. His expression was grim, and he carried a tablet in one hand. "Sorry to keep you waiting. It took time to review the footage from the security cameras at the car mechanic's shop, but I have something to show you." He propped the tablet up against the wall. "The footage is grainy, and the attacker keeps his face turned away from the camera, but pay close attention to the way he moves. It might be familiar to you."

Willow nodded, her heart picking up speed as Chief Garcia hit play on the screen. The attacker was dressed in black, a hoodie pulled over his head to block his face. He stealthily approached her SUV and disappeared under the carriage. Three minutes later, he reappeared and strolled for the sidewalk, hands in his pockets, as if he was meandering through the park on a Sunday.

The callousness of his behavior was appalling. Anger burst through Willow. "He planted that bomb without a moment's hesitation. What kind of person does that?"

"A murderer." Logan glared at the tablet screen. "A cold-blooded one."

He was right. Whoever planted the bomb had probably also shot her bodyguard. Willow took a deep breath to steady her emotions. "Can you play the video again, Chief? I'd like to take another look."

"We can watch it as many times as you need." He tapped the screen again.

This time, Willow paid close attention to the man as the chief instructed, but nothing about him was familiar. "I don't recognize him." She turned to Logan. "Do you?"

He shook his head. "No." He pushed out a breath of frustration. "There isn't any other security camera footage of him? Maybe from some of the shops on the street?"

"Unfortunately not." Chief Garcia flipped off the tablet. "We found fresh tire tracks in the alley next to the mechanic's shop. My guess is the bomber parked there. I've had deputies scour the area for evidence, but we've come up empty-handed. The bomb fragments, along with the SUV, have been sent to the state crime lab. It'll take time to get their reports."

"Can you tell us anything about the bomb?" Logan asked. "What was it made of?"

"At a preliminary glance, it was constructed using

common household materials, like fertilizer. The bomber connected it to the SUV's engine. It was designed to explode once the vehicle started." His expression turned grim. "It was incredibly fortunate you started the SUV via your remote."

Logan crossed his arms over his chest. "So anyone with access to the internet and a basic understanding of vehicles could've made and installed the bomb."

"Yes. Due to the serious nature of these attacks on Willow, I've requested help from the Texas Rangers. Ranger Grady West will be here tomorrow morning. I've worked with him before. He's detail oriented and thorough."

The chief was doing everything he could to speed up the investigation, but Willow knew from listening to her uncle that the wheels of justice often moved at a snail's pace. She rubbed her forehead. A headache was forming at the base of her skull, wrapping tight tentacles around her temples. "Who is doing this? And why?" She dropped her hand to study the lawman across the table. "Have you been able to track down every criminal on the list Uncle Scott gave you?"

"Yes. So far, there's no evidence linking these attacks to your uncle's time as a federal prosecutor."

Willow's heart sank. "So then Senator Randall may truly be behind this." She pushed away from the table and rose. "All of this to win an election? It's sickening."

"Hold on." Chief Garcia raised a hand. "I'm aware of Senator Randall's reputation, but we can't jump to conclusions. There's no evidence linking him to any of these crimes either." His gaze jumped between Willow and

Logan. "Unless you've uncovered something I don't know about."

"Nothing that can be used in a court of law, but yes." Logan frowned. "My buddy Jason went to interview Ken Watson."

"The newspaper reporter?"

"Former newspaper reporter, yes. Ken was investigating claims of racketeering. Senator Randall was supposedly taking money in exchange for his vote on certain legislation." Logan's mouth flattened into a thin line. "Ken was repeatedly threatened while working on the story. His house was broken into. Photographs of his wife were used for target practice and then mailed to his office. He also received nasty phone calls and texts. The last straw was when someone kidnapped his five-year-old during a birthday party."

Willow gasped. "Please tell me the poor baby is okay."

"Yes. The kidnapper locked the kid in a closet. When they found her, a note was pinned to the back of her shirt ordering Ken to stop the investigation or else. As you can imagine, it scared the wits out of Ken and his wife. He quit his job the next day." Logan pinned Chief Garcia with a look. "The Austin Police Department investigated but never found any evidence linking Senator Randall to the threats against Ken."

Chief Garcia sighed. "But he's convinced there's a link."

"He is. Ken's terrified of Randall to this day and has refused to speak to law enforcement further. He initially didn't want to talk to Jason either, but finally gave in once he heard about the threats against Willow."

Her knees became rubbery as the stark magnitude of

what she was facing became crystal clear. Willow gripped the back of the chair for support. "If Randall was behind the threats against Ken, he didn't kidnap the kid himself. Or send the threats. He hired someone to do it."

"Yes, I believe that's exactly what we're dealing with." He pointed to the tablet. "Whoever planted that bomb was polished. He moved without hesitation. Former military, maybe? Special ops, in my opinion. He was careful and deliberate. The attack on Willow in the Blessed Hearts parking lot, and the murder of her bodyguard, were also well-planned." Logan's gaze narrowed. "Randall wouldn't hire an amateur. There's too much risk if something goes wrong."

Willow's stomach clenched. Having her life threatened by a stranger was scary enough, but if she was the target of a professional killer... that was horrifying. It also didn't quite sit right. Her mind whirled, thinking over the attacks. "Would a hired hitman pay off my bodyguard? Or send me a threatening text?" She used shaky fingers to brush her bangs out of her eyes. "I would assume he'd just kill me and have it over with. It doesn't make sense."

"It does if the orders are simply to terrify you until your uncle quits the race." Logan tilted his head. "Senator Randall can't go around killing anyone who dares to question him. He can, however, intimidate them into silence. He uses an enforcer. Someone on his payroll who will take care of his problems. A man who uses various methods—like physical altercations or sending threatening texts—to get his point across."

Willow wrapped her arms around herself. She was ice

cold. Thunder from the storm rattled the window. "And the bombing today? Was that designed to frighten me?"

"Perhaps." Logan's brow creased. "The bomber had no way of knowing when or if we'd pick up your car from the shop. The mechanic could've needed to move the SUV for some reason, which would've triggered the explosion. Or, more likely, your uncle would've sent a bodyguard to retrieve the car. In the end, the result would've been the same. We'd believe your life was in danger."

"It is." White-hot anger flooded her veins, washing away the icy chill of fear. "And not just mine. Multiple people could've been killed in the bombing today. Innocent people. I don't like being treated like a pawn in some twisted game. If Senator Randall is behind this, he needs to be in prison."

"If is the key word in that sentence," Chief Garcia said. "We need to use caution here. There's no direct evidence Senator Randall is behind these threats. We can't even be certain that these attacks are being carried out by a hitman or that they're connected to the campaign. This could be personal."

"What do you mean?"

"Your family was well known, even before Scott started running for senate. Seeing y'all in the news could've triggered someone who felt wronged by something done in the past." Chief Garcia shrugged. "I'm sorry to say it, but people have been targeted over road rage incidents."

"Chief, this is calculated," Logan interjected. "And personal. Whoever is behind these threats put some planning into it."

"You could both be right." Willow sighed. "Buchanan's

Grocery was sold after my parents died. There were layoffs shortly thereafter. The family received threats back then, although my uncle did his best to shield me from it. Eventually things died down. But that's just one example of how my family has affected others. There's no way to know if someone is seeking vengeance against us for some perceived injustice. Right now, we have a lot of questions and not many answers."

"Agreed." Chief Garcia's phone beeped with a text message. He glanced at the screen. "I'm sorry, there's an issue that needs my attention. Please excuse me."

He hurried from the room. The door closed with a snick behind him.

Fear descended on Willow with fierce claws. The thunderstorm continued to rage, the wind lashing at the trees. She shivered. Her feet, of their own accord, crossed the room to the window. Rain beat against the glass.

Was the killer out there right now? Watching her?

Willow felt rather than heard Logan come up behind her. He placed his hands on her shoulders. "It's going to be okay."

She nearly laughed. "Okay? A bomb was placed in my car today. Things are far from okay." Willow didn't recognize her own voice. It was hollow. Empty. This was a place she recognized well. After losing her parents, she'd wrapped herself in numbness to ease the pain. "My life is being turned upside down, and there's nothing I can do to stop it."

Logan gently turned her toward him and then tilted a finger under her chin, lifting her face until her eyes met his. "You aren't in this alone."

The understanding and compassion buried in their depths nearly caused a sob to rise up in her chest. Willow battled it back. There were things that needed to be said. "When you agreed to be my bodyguard, the threat wasn't this serious. You have a family to think of. Mia. I wouldn't blame you one bit if you backed out now, Logan."

He placed a finger against her lips. Willow's breath caught.

Logan held her gaze. "Thank you for thinking of my family, but it's not necessary. I knew the risks when I accepted the mission. Nothing has changed. I'm in this."

TEN

The threats against Willow weighed heavily on Logan throughout the next day and into the evening. He'd accompanied her to work, and all had been quiet thankfully, but it didn't ease his worry. The killer was out there somewhere, planning his next move. Logan could feel it.

He adjusted his tie before smoothing down the collar of his shirt. Nerves jittered his stomach. This evening was Scott's birthday party. Paintings, done by the teens at Blessed Hearts, would be auctioned off. The proceeds would go toward the youth center's outdoor recreational center.

It was a brilliant fundraising move, but the party created a logistical nightmare. He'd spent most of the day studying blueprints with Nathan and Kyle, who were also attending the event. They'd created a security plan that included several escape routes. Bodyguards hired by Scott would also be on the premises. There would be several layers of protection.

Logan prayed it was enough.

He shrugged on his suit jacket, checked his reflection one more time, and then headed into the hall. Mia's bedroom door was open. The teen was seated at her desk, head bent over a notebook, dark hair hiding her face. A stack of school books rested at her elbow. Her computer screen was dark.

"What are you working on?" Logan asked.

"Math homework. I have a test next week." Mia barely glanced up as she shoved a strand of hair behind her ear. She stuck the eraser end of the pencil into her mouth absently as she studied the open school book in front of her. The notebook held math equations with several smudges left over by the eraser.

Shock rippled through Logan. Mia hadn't done a lick of homework without being bugged, pleaded, or blackmailed since her parents died. He was half tempted to check her temperature to make sure the teen was okay. Instead, he tamped down his initial reaction and kept his tone casual. "Need any help?"

"Do you understand quadratic equations?"

"Sure do."

He spent the next twenty minutes walking her through several example problems. It was clear working with the tutor at Blessed Hearts was having an effect on his niece. She was engaged, and asked questions. Logan couldn't be more overjoyed. It was a small change, yes, but it was a step in the right direction. It gave him hope.

Mia grinned broadly when she worked the last equation on her own. "Yes! Finally, I understand. I'm going to finish the rest of these problems and then do my English essay." She sat back in her chair. "Thanks, Uncle Logan."

"Anytime." He rose from his perch on her rolling drawer stand before shoving the furniture back under the desk where it belonged. "I'm heading out now, but Papa and Nana are downstairs."

"Okay." Mia eyed him. "You look nice, by the way."

"Thanks."

He turned to leave, but Mia called his name. Logan turned back. "Yeah."

"I like her. Ms. Cassidy, I mean." She shrugged. "Just in case you were wondering."

For the second time, Logan was caught off guard. He was speechless for a moment, trying to sort out the mixture of feelings rumbling around inside him. His romantic relationship with Willow wasn't real. They'd both agreed on that. And yet, he couldn't deny that something was developing between them. Did he want to continue a relationship with her after this was all over? Did she want to date him?

It was too much to consider at the moment. Logan shoved the questions aside and focused on Mia. "I'm glad you like her. We're keeping things light for the moment, getting to know each other better."

He didn't want Mia to be disappointed when the relationship didn't work out, but it touched him that she'd taken the time to express her approval. If nothing else, Logan intended to maintain a friendship with Willow. She was also someone Mia could turn to. "You know, Willow lost her parents when she was thirteen. If you need someone to talk to, someone who can understand what it's like, she's a good option."

"I'll think about it." Mia turned back to her books. "Have a good night."

"You too." Logan hesitated, then crossed the room and kissed the top of her head. "Love you, kid."

He went downstairs, said goodbye to his parents, and stepped out into the crisp fall air. It smelled of damp grass and dried leaves. The drive to Willow's house only took fifteen minutes. Logan collected the bouquet he'd purchased along the way and got out of his Jeep. The space between his shoulder blades itched as he took the steps to the front porch. There were eyes on him. Jason and Walker were guarding the house and had probably noticed his arrival.

Logan rang the bell. A peel of laughter came from inside, followed by the sound of footsteps moments before the door swung open wide. Addison, Jason's wife, stood in the entryway. Her cheeks were flushed, her auburn hair flowing past her shoulders, a grin on her face. Beyond her, a gaggle of women's voices ebbed and flowed. Someone cheered.

Addison grabbed Logan by the wrist and tugged him inside. Normally, the family law attorney dressed in attire suitable for court. Tonight, however, she wore a T-shirt and jeans. Her feet were bare. "Great, you're here. Willow is almost ready." She released him, eyed the flowers, and clapped. "Oh, those are gorgeous."

Logan's cheeks heated. The plastic crinkled as his grip around the bouquet tightened. "Ummm, not to sound rude or anything, but what are you doing here, Addison?"

"The ladies and I came to help Willow get ready for her date tonight." She glanced behind her and lowered her voice. "She's a gem, Logan. I couldn't be happier for you."

The compliment was heartfelt, and it sent a zing of guilt straight through Logan. He hated lying to his friends and Mia. The last thing he wanted was to hurt them. This relationship with Willow was getting more complicated by the moment and he didn't know how to slow it down. Or even if he wanted to. It was a confusing mess.

Before he could muster a response, a pack of women flooded out of the back bedroom. Cassie, Nathan's wife, her blonde hair pulled back into a ponytail, greeted him with a hug. She was followed by Sierra, who hitched her adopted nephew higher on her hip.

"Uncle Logan." Daniel grinned, a tiny dimple appearing in his cheek, and reached for Logan.

He handed the flowers to Sierra before lifting the little boy in his arms. "Hey there, buddy. Good to see you."

Leah, Tucker's wife, carried a set of dirty plates past him, heading for the kitchen. The new bride was fresh off her honeymoon and glowed with happiness. "Hi, Logan. There's some leftover pie if you want a slice."

"Pie? You guys brought pie?"

"Of course we did." Addison waved off his question with a flick of her hand. "Did you think we'd neglect to introduce Willow to the best pie in Texas? Once Harriet and Nelson learned we were coming to hang out with her, they gave us an assortment of flavors." Her eyes sparkled with mischief. "Apparently, a little birdie told them you and Willow were dating. They send their love."

Logan nearly groaned. Harriet and Nelson owned a diner off a quiet country road. It was where Logan and his friends met on Wednesdays for their unofficial support group meetings. The food was outstanding and their homemade pies couldn't be beat. Over time, the older couple had become an adopted set of grandparents for all the guys. Logan would have a lot of explaining to do next time he went to Nelson's Diner.

Daniel wriggled, trying to climb up Logan's chest to hang from his shoulder. The little boy was daring. It probably didn't help that he was growing up with a crew of "uncles" who loved to roughhouse.

Logan shifted his hold. He was so caught up in trying to keep the kid from falling headfirst to the ground, he didn't hear Willow come into the room, but something inside him sensed her presence anyway. He looked up.

His heart stuttered. Willow's black dress clung to her curves, the hemline kissing her calves at an asymmetrical angle. Heels added a few inches of height to her petite frame. Her lips were a deep, kissable red, which popped against her porcelain skin and blonde hair. She'd kept the rest of her makeup simple, but nothing could diminish the stunning color of her eyes. They were ocean blue. Deep enough to drown a man.

No, not just any man. Him. He could drown in them.

Logan's mouth went dry and his brain froze. The women were talking, but he didn't register a word of what they were saying. It was only when Sierra plucked Daniel from his arms that Logan tore his gaze away from Willow. In the next moment, the flowers were back in his hand.

Someone pushed him gently. The sound of laughter followed.

Say something!

He was standing like a dolt in the middle of the entryway. Logan blinked. He took a deep breath and forced his brain to operate his mouth. "You look... amazing." He thrust the flowers toward Willow. "These are for you."

Real smooth, Keller.

She blushed, taking them. "Thank you." Then she moved closer, rose on her tiptoes, and brushed a kiss across his cheek. Her breath was warm against his ear as she whispered, "You look very handsome."

His pulse rate skyrocketed. It was sheer strength of will that kept Logan from wrapping his arms around Willow and pulling her close for a proper kiss. The scent of her perfume was driving him mad, the nearness of her body sending all his cells on alert. Somewhere in the back of his mind, Logan registered they had an audience. Willow was simply playing the part of his girlfriend, but that fact didn't cut through the desire coursing through him.

He was in trouble. Deep trouble.

"Our work is done here, ladies." Addison's voice was full of glee. "Let's go. Willow, it was fun. We'll talk again soon. Bye, Logan."

The women piled out of the house, their voices and giggles carrying even through the closed front door.

Willow's blush deepened. She lifted the flowers slightly. "I should put these in water before we go."

"Right."

He followed her into the kitchen. Pie boxes were piled next to the trash can in the corner. A few leftover slices were set aside on a plate and covered with plastic wrap. Logan shoved his hands in his pockets, feeling unusually awkward. "I'm sorry about the bombardment. I didn't know the women were coming over today or I would've warned you."

"Nonsense." Willow pulled a vase from the pantry and filled it with water. "Your friends are wonderful. It was really nice having them here. I haven't laughed that hard in a long time."

She set the flowers in the vase and smiled. "These are gorgeous. You didn't have to bring me flowers." Willow sent him a teasing look. "I have a feeling your buddies are going to get an earful tonight from their significant others."

He laughed. "You're right. I love their wives to pieces, but news travels fast in this group. It doesn't help that Addison has been on a mission to marry me off for months. Poor Walker. She's going to turn all her attention toward him now."

They both laughed. Willow set the vase on the table and checked her watch. "Oh, we'd better get moving. Give me just a second to grab my purse and coat."

Logan waited patiently for her in the entryway. He glanced out the window next to the front door. The street was quiet. Jason and Walker were still standing guard. They'd let him know if anyone attempted to approach the house. Willow's footsteps preceded her into the room.

He turned. Instantly, Logan knew something was wrong. Willow was pale as a ghost and shaking. She held her cell phone in one hand with a white-knuckled grip. He closed the distance between them. "What is it? Another text?"

She nodded. Logan wrapped an arm around Willow's waist, pulling her trembling body up next to his, and then tilted her phone screen in order to read the text. His blood boiled.

I'm watching. You won't know when, you won't know how, but I'm coming for you.

ELEVEN

The birthday party was in full swing as Willow entered the foyer of her uncle's house. The hour-long drive had done little to settle her nerves, but Logan's steady presence did. He looked sharp in his dark blue suit. The jacket molded to his broad shoulders and the crisp white shirt accented his olive complexion. More than one woman cast him an appreciative glance as Willow checked her coat at a small alcove next to the entrance. She could hardly blame them. He was breathtaking.

Logan arched his brows as she accepted the ticket from the woman behind the counter. "Your uncle has a coat check? I thought that only existed in restaurants or fancy hotels."

"Kathryn designed the house with parties in mind." Willow wrinkled her nose. "Entertaining is one thing, but she takes it to another level. I don't know how my uncle keeps up. At one point, she was having an event a week."

She tucked the ticket in her purse, next to her cell phone. She'd also shoved her pepper spray inside the bag as well. It hadn't prevented the attack in the parking lot, but she hated the idea of being completely defenseless.

Logan offered his arm, and she slipped her hand into the crook of his elbow. They strolled across the black-and-white tile floor. A chandelier cast light across the double staircase leading to the second floor. Beyond the foyer was a large formal living room with floor-to-ceiling windows that'd been cast open to allow access to the extensive backyard.

Easels with paintings were strategically placed around the living room. Several had gold lettered SOLD signs attached to them. Willow's worry gave way to happiness. "Look at how many paintings have been bought. I'm so excited."

"I can't believe these were done by teens." Logan moved from easel to easel. "The kids at the youth center are extremely talented. I can barely draw a stick figure."

Willow laughed. "Me too." She stopped in front of a winter landscape with barren trees and a frozen river. It was austere and stark, yet there was a glow of light emanating from the darkness. It was entitled Hope. "This one is especially touching. The first time I saw it, I fell in love."

Logan studied the painting for a moment. "I can see why. Things can look so bleak, but the light in the corner is a reminder that God's love is always there."

"Yes. I couldn't have said it better myself."

Their gazes met and her heart skipped a beat. The moment stretched out, the air between them crackling with electricity that was both exhilarating and unsettling. Logan saw her. He got her. Willow had never experienced this kind of connection with a man before. She wanted desperately to trust it but wasn't sure she could. Hadn't they agreed this was all an act?

Confused, she stepped away from Logan and headed for the backyard. "We should say hello to my uncle."

He followed, catching up quickly. Guests mingled around the buffet table. Three separate bars were scattered around the space. Music spilled from the six-member orchestra, mingling with the din of voices. A three-layer birthday cake encrusted with jewels sat on one end of a table. On the other was an ice sculpture of a mermaid. Champagne spilled in a constant stream from the jar in her hands. Twinkling lights spread elegantly around the space gave an intimate ambience.

It was beautiful. Willow wasn't a fan of fancy parties, but Uncle Scott would be touched by the effort Kathryn had made. That was the most important part.

Her gaze skimmed over the guests. Kyle, dressed in a suit, chatted with his cousin Nathan in a rear corner. Both men appeared relaxed, each with a drink in their hand, but their attention never settled in one place for too long. Beyond the twinkling lights of the backyard, bodyguards paced the perimeter. The house was practically a fortress.

She spotted her uncle talking to the mayor of Knoxville. Willow began moving in his direction but didn't have to go far. Scott met them halfway. He greeted her with a warm hug before shaking Logan's hand.

"Happy birthday." Willow smiled. She was very aware their interaction was being watched by many of the guests. Worry lurked in Scott's eyes when he looked at her. He'd been in constant contact with Willow since the explosion but didn't know about the latest text message. And she wasn't planning on telling him. Not tonight. "Another year older, but you only get more handsome."

Scott snorted. "There's no need to lie. I'm getting more gray hair by the minute." His expression warmed. "You're the spitting image of your mom. I wish your parents could see you now. They'd be so proud of you."

Willow squeezed her uncle's arm. She missed her parents dearly and often wondered if they'd be proud of the woman she'd become. Scott never failed to tell her they would. It was nice to hear. "Kathryn has outdone herself. Everything looks amazing."

"She's been planning the party for weeks. Speaking of my lovely wife, she needs to speak to you. I think she's in the library handling some last-minute campaign issues." Scott frowned. "If you can, wrangle her out here to enjoy the party. Business can wait for one night."

"I will." Willow patted his arm one more time before turning to head back inside.

Logan placed a hand on the small of her back and tilted his head closer to hers. "Any idea what your aunt wants to discuss?"

"Probably the bombing. It was in the national news today and I'm sure Kathryn wants to capitalize on it."

Willow wasn't looking forward to the discussion. Chances were, her aunt wanted her to do an interview. She had no intention of complying. While Willow fully supported her uncle, she didn't enjoy being the center of attention. The text messages from the killer were terrifying enough as it was. She was quickly becoming some kind of obsession for him.

It took time to cross the living room and foyer. Willow

was stopped several times by guests and got stuck in small talk. She introduced Logan, and overall, everyone was very polite. A few questions about the attacks came up in conversation, but she deftly avoided answering them.

As they slipped into the hall behind the double staircase, Logan blew out a breath. "You handled that very well. I don't think I could've navigated those questions with as much grace."

She smiled up at him. "One of the best lessons my grandmother ever taught me was to turn the conversation around by asking someone about themselves. People like it when you show a genuine interest in them. It has the added bonus of taking the heat off you when troublesome questions come up."

"Huh. I'll have to remember that the next time Addison bugs me about my dating life."

Willow burst out laughing. "I should add a caveat. The trick doesn't work with someone like Addison. She knows how to cut right through the nonsense and get to the heart of the matter."

Logan arched his brow. "Uh-oh. What kinds of questions did she ask you earlier tonight?"

"Nothing I couldn't handle." Heat infused her cheeks. Addison hadn't been pushy, but Willow also hadn't been able to hide her true feelings for Logan. Of course, it fit with the narrative that he was her boyfriend, but the depth of her emotions had been surprising. And Addison had noticed.

Shaking off her train of thought, Willow focused on the task in front of her. The library door was cocked open, so she didn't bother to knock before entering. Logan followed.

Tall bookcases graced three of the four walls. A desk

was set in front of a picture window overlooking the back garden. Overstuffed leather couches were arranged around a fireplace. The room smelled of old books and cigar smoke.

Kathryn stood facing the door, dressed in a glittery form-fitting pantsuit with a daring back and a modest front. Her makeup was perfect, hair tucked into a chignon. Tendrils drifted around her elegant features.

She handed a man on the couch a drink. His back was to Willow, but she had a clear view of Kathryn's flirtatious smile and the man's hand as he took the glass, lingering far longer than was necessary, his thumb caressing her aunt's skin. Words were exchanged but spoken too low to carry across the room.

There was nothing overt, nothing glaringly obvious, but Willow suddenly felt like she'd intruded on a private moment. An intimate one.

Then Kathryn glanced up. The air in the room shifted so quickly, Willow convinced herself that she'd imagined the entire exchange.

"There you are, Willow. Finally." Kathryn waved her forward. "We have a lot to discuss in a short time. I want you to meet the new strategist I hired this afternoon. Mike has some fresh ideas on how to handle the media coverage regarding the recent attacks."

Willow's steps faltered as the man seated on the leather couch rose. Mike Jensen. Her ex-boyfriend. The man who'd torn out her heart and made a fool of her. Shock stilled her tongue.

"Hello, Willow." Mike offered a smarmy smile full of cockiness and satisfaction. "It's good to see you again."

Logan's gaze shot from Mike to her, and then back again. "You two know each other?"

Mike lifted the glass of whiskey in his hand and took a sip. "We used to date. It was a long time ago."

Five years. A lifetime ago, and yet the pain of his betrayal still stung. Back then, he'd been a scrappy pre-law student with a burning desire to put criminals behind bars. His family was blue collar and down to earth. Money, or so Willow mistakenly thought, didn't matter to him.

Time had obviously changed Mike's circumstances. His suit was designer, as were his shoes. An oversized watch, etched with diamonds, decorated one wrist. His dark hair was styled with gel in the latest fashion. He looked smoothed and polished. Confident. But underneath all of that was still the same man as before. A user.

Willow fixed her attention on Kathryn. "I don't know what Mike has told you, but I have no intention of working with him on anything. I would also strongly advise that you fire him from the campaign immediately."

"That's impossible. Scott's poll numbers are not where they need to be. These death threats are taking up far too much of the media's attention, robbing him of valuable air time to get his message across to constituents. Mike is one of the best strategists in the state. We're fortunate to have him." Kathryn folded her hands together. "I realize the two of you had a romantic relationship once, but surely we can all be adults and work together for Scott's benefit."

"Mike's only interest is himself." Willow crossed her arms over her chest. "He won't be loyal to Uncle Scott."

Kathryn's nostrils flared. Her aunt had never handled being contradicted well. "I see your emotions are getting the better of you, Willow. Let's table this discussion for another time." Her tone was ice cold. "Tonight is Scott's birthday. We should all enjoy the party."

"I couldn't agree more." Mike set down his empty whiskey glass and offered his arm to Kathryn. "Allow me."

Mike shot Willow a smirk over his shoulder before disappearing around the corner. Her blood boiled in response. How could she have ever found him attractive?

Logan shut the library door and then turned toward Willow. "I take it you didn't know your ex was in town."

"Not a clue. The man's a manipulative snake." She blew out a breath. Logan couldn't understand the gravity of the matter without explaining the entire story. "We dated for over nine months. I thought we were in love, headed toward engagement and marriage, until one night I overheard him bragging to a buddy. Mike was running a long con on me. He wanted access to my uncle's connections and my trust fund."

Embarrassment and shame rose inside her. "I've been taken advantage of before by so-called friends. People who were more interested in my wealth than in me. But I'd developed a kind of radar for it over the years. Somehow, Mike slipped past all my defenses. I never saw the truth. He had me convinced it was love."

Hot tears pricked the back of her eyes. Horrified, Willow dipped her head to swipe at them. Mike didn't deserve one ounce of her sadness. She was better off without him—there was no doubt about that—but he'd broken her trust. She'd put up barriers in response, knowing that her own judgment couldn't be relied on.

Logan came to stand in front of her. He placed his

hands on her shoulders, his touch gentle as he pulled her in for a hug. "Mike's a fool. You're so much more than the money in your bank account or your family's connections. Smart. Compassionate. Giving. Brave." He let out a light chuckle. "A teen whisperer. Mia was doing her homework today when I left the house."

Willow's head shot up. "Really?"

"Really." Warmth darkened the color of his eyes to a deep brown. "We haven't known each other long, but you've done nothing but impress me at every turn."

Her breath hitched. It was the most heartfelt and genuine compliment she'd ever received. Once again, the notion that Logan saw her in a way no one else had before washed over her. Willow was suddenly aware of the closeness of their bodies. His muscular arms enveloped her, the heat of his hands seeping through the fabric of her dress. The smell of his aftershave drew her closer. Butterflies rioted in her stomach as her gaze dropped to his mouth.

It would be irresponsible to kiss Logan. A recipe for heartbreak. But at that moment, Willow couldn't bring herself to move away from him. She rose on her toes as Logan bent his head to meet her halfway. His breath touched her face just as the lights went out, suddenly casting the room into darkness.

Willow froze, a cold dose of fear erasing the heat of her desire. "What happened?"

A series of explosions erupted, rattling the panes in the glass window.

Then came the screams.

TWELVE

"We're under attack." Kyle's tone was clipped. Screaming and the sounds of chaos filtered through the open phone line. "Several smoke bombs went off and there's mass panic. Where are you?"

"Library. West wing." Logan glanced at Willow huddled beside him behind the desk. Her complexion was pale, eyes wide with fear. In her hand, she gripped a can of pepper spray.

Logan wanted to comfort her, but he held his gun in one hand and his cell in the other. The best way to help Willow was to keep her safe. Smoke bombs contained chemicals. They weren't designed to emit sparks, but were still a hazard if something nearby was flammable. "Can we stay put? Is the house on fire?"

"Unknown," Kyle replied. "There's a lot of smoke, some of it's gray."

Not good. Smoke bombs used colored vapor. Gray smoke meant something was burning, and Logan had to assume the house was on fire. Given the size of the mansion, it could take time for the flames to reach them, but there was no way to be certain. They had to get out now. "Affirmative. Heading to the rendezvous point. Any tangos?"

"None visible. Nathan and I are moving in your direction, but we've got injured here. The hired bodyguards bailed faster than the civilians."

"Affirmative." Logan didn't need further explanation. Nathan and Kyle had a duty to protect innocent people, not just Willow. They couldn't leave the injured civilians to face down an unknown enemy. "I've got this. Stay safe."

He hung up. Logan quickly ran through different scenarios in his mind based on what he knew about the layout of the house and rejected most of them. The easiest way to escape would be via the side yard. It wasn't the most strategic—they would be out in the open—but he didn't know where the fire was. The last thing Logan wanted to do was lead them into a worse situation.

He adjusted the hold on his handgun. "Does that window open?"

"Yes." Willow pointed to the middle section. "There's a latch that releases the entire section from the ceiling to the ledge."

"Okay, this is what's going to happen. You stay here while I open the window. After I determine it's safe, you'll crawl over to me. We'll go into the yard and then run for the woods along the edge of the property. You don't look back and you don't stop, no matter what you hear. Once you're inside the tree line, wait for me. We'll go to the car together."

She frowned. "Heading to the woods would mean we'd be going the wrong way. Your Jeep is next to the kitchen."

"No, it isn't. Nathan hid it at the edge of the property earlier." Logan pulled the keys from his pocket and pressed them into her hand. "If something happens to me, you need to keep moving. Do not under any circumstances try to help me. Is that understood?"

"I don't understand..." Her chin trembled. "What's going to happen to you?"

Logan didn't want to explain the variables running through his head. Years in the military had taught him to think like a tango. The smoke bombs served two possible purposes. One was to create chaos and confusion so the attacker could grab Willow. The other was to drive them from the house so he could pick them off with a sniper's rifle. Logan prayed the former was the killer's plan, but he couldn't rely on that.

He met her gaze. Half her face was hidden in shadows. The only illumination filtering into the room was from the window. Moonlight caressed her cheek and swept across her blonde hair. Logan gave in to temptation and cupped her chin. Willow's skin was silky under his fingertips. "I'm a trained warrior. Don't worry about me. Just do as I say and everything will be fine. Understood?"

She hesitated and then nodded. With regret, Logan released her. He wanted to kiss her, but now was not the time. His gaze went to the window and the yard beyond. There was half a football field between their location and the woods.

Please Lord, watch over us.

Willow grabbed his arm, halting him from moving toward the window. "Wait." She lifted her hand and cupped the back of his neck, pulling him down until his lips were pressed against hers.

The initial surprise gave way to an immediate burst of desire. Logan wrapped his arms around Willow, drawing her closer. Time stopped as his world narrowed to the woman in his arms. The feel of her soft lips against his, the touch of her fingers against the nape of his neck, the swell of emotions rising inside him. He'd tangled himself in knots to avoid the truth that she freed with one kiss.

There was something deep happening between them. Something profound. Something that would change the course of his life.

Logan broke off the kiss, breathless, his mind muddled. He sucked in air. "I can't rescue you, woman, if you distract me with kisses that shut off my brain."

Her pretty mouth curved into a smile. "Sorry."

He kissed her once more, hard and fast, then released her. He took another deep breath to clear his thoughts. It took another few precious seconds to snap back into soldier mode. He had to get them out of there.

Logan adjusted the grip on his handgun and belly crawled to the window. The library was on the opposite side of the house from the primary location of the party. If guests had fled this way while escaping the attack, they weren't visible. Logan reached up and unlocked the window. It creaked open on the hinges. There was no screen, probably because it was designed to roll down via remote control.

Frigid air washed over his heated skin. Logan scanned the woods and surrounding area for any movement. Nothing stirred. That didn't comfort him. Whoever was after Willow had proven to be adept at striking when the moment was right.

Logan lifted another prayer to the good Lord before gesturing Willow to join him at the window. Seconds later, she was at his side. She'd removed her heels and held them in one hand. Logan assisted her over the window ledge. A cloud drifted across the moon, casting everything in shadow. "Run. Now."

She bolted across the grass. He held his weapon at the ready, covering her escape. His heart thundered faster with every step she took toward the woods. It wasn't until Willow disappeared into the shelter of the trees that he let out the breath he was holding.

She was safe. For now.

He vaulted over the ledge, his dress shoes sinking into the grass. Adrenaline poured through his veins. Logan kept his weapon handy as he ran across the yard. The cloud shifted again and moonlight flooded the open area. A shadow moved in the tree line. The glint of a rifle caught his attention. Logan had seconds to divert course toward a decorative well before shots rang out.

He dove behind the brick structure. Rolling, he came up to one knee, cupping his weapon in both hands. He returned fire. The assailant responded by unleashing a spray of bullets. Logan ducked down. Bullets slammed into the well. Pieces of brick and mortar peppered his face and body. There was nothing he could do but take cover. He was outgunned.

Something hot streaked across his calf, cutting through his pants and searing his skin. Logan pulled the limb closer, his hand automatically covering the wound. Blood seeped between his fingers.

He'd been hit. How badly he couldn't tell. Another dark cloud swept across the moon. He prayed Willow had listened to instructions and was headed for the Jeep. As long as the assailant was shooting at Logan, he wasn't going after her.

Silence descended. Heart pounding, Logan took a deep breath to clear his mind of the pain and counteract the adrenaline narrowing his vision. He tore a strip of fabric from his shirt and wrapped it around the gunshot. It was a flimsy bandage, but it was better than nothing. Then he poked his head above the brick structure. The gunman had shifted position. He was a dark shadow, barely visible among the tree line.

Logan steadied his breath, raised his weapon, and took a shot.

The sound of a grunt carried across the distance between them, followed by a fresh spray of bullets. Once again, Logan took cover until the shooting stopped. When he peered over the well again, the assailant was gone.

"Oh no, you don't."

Logan shot up. His calf roared in protest, fiery heat nearly taking him back down to the ground again, but he gritted his teeth against the pain and kept moving. His job was to protect Willow at all costs. The woman wore a cocktail gown and high heels. That wasn't the best attire for a run through the woods. There was no way to know if she'd reached the Jeep yet. He wouldn't risk the gunman catching up to her.

Darkness shrouded Logan as he entered the woods.

Branches tore at his clothes and scraped his face. He kept his ears pricked for any sound of the attacker, but it was difficult to hear over the pounding of his own heart. The man could be anywhere.

A root tripped him and Logan stumbled. His hand shot out, grasping a tree limb to stop his fall. His dress shoes were appropriate for a fancy party, but they had little to no traction. He mentally berated himself for not wearing his combat boots. Not fashionable, but far better for an encounter with a killer.

Logan sucked in another deep breath and kept moving. His calf was still bleeding, the fluid seeping through the fabric of his bandage and dripping into his sock. The pain barely cut through the surge of worry compelling him forward.

He couldn't let Willow down. He wouldn't.

THIRTEEN

She couldn't get air into her lungs.

Willow bolted through the woods like a hunted deer. Thorns and exposed roots stabbed her bare feet. The pain barely registered. Survival instinct was driving her forward. The attacker had attempted to nab her. Willow wriggled free of his grasp, but she was under no illusions that he would give up.

He was coming for her.

She dared a glance over her shoulder. No one was there. The stitch in her side made her want to throw up. How much farther could she run? Willow clutched the can of pepper spray in one hand, Logan's car keys in the other. If she could make it to the Jeep, then there was a fighting chance. For her. And for Logan.

Was he alive? She desperately prayed he was. The attacker had pelted Logan's hiding place with bullets before she'd been able to devise a plan to distract him. It'd been reckless and more than stupid to attack the gunman on her own armed with a tree branch and a can of pepper spray, but she'd been desperate. The thought of losing Logan... it was heart-wrenching. She couldn't stand by and let him die.

Willow burst out of the woods onto a dirt road running along the backside of her uncle's property. The Jeep was parked a short distance away. Relief weakened her knees. Her heart thundered in her ears and she bent over to catch her breath. Sweat slicked her skin. One minute. She just needed one minute.

A cold barrel touched the back of her neck.

"Don't move."

She froze. Goosebumps pebbled across her skin, despite the warmth generated from her race through the woods. Rocks bit into her bare soles. Moonlight filtered through the trees, illuminating Logan's vehicle. So close and yet too far away.

She willed her mind to push away the fear. If the attacker wanted her dead, he would've shot her already.

"I..." She heaved. "...can't breathe."

Willow sank to the ground on her knees. She placed her finger over the button of her pepper spray and drew in as deep of a breath as she dared. The hitman growled and cursed. He bent to grab her arm.

She whipped her hand up and sprayed him in the face.

He screamed. He released her and backed up. A string of curses followed.

Tears flooded her own vision, and she gagged as some of the pepper spray hit her in the face as well. Willow stumbled to her feet. It wasn't possible for her to drive now. She abandoned the idea of heading for Logan's vehicle and dove back into the woods. Her eyes burned. The pain was some of the worst she'd ever felt. Still, Willow kept moving forward.

A set of arms wrapped around her. One clapped over her mouth, the other around her waist.

He'd caught her.

She panicked, rearing back trying to break his nose with her head. Fear stole what little breath she had left. Tears streamed down her face.

"Stop, Willow. It's me."

Logan's voice cut through her fear. She sagged against him, sobs building in her chest. He lifted his hand from her mouth and placed a finger against his lips to indicate she should be quiet. It took every ounce of self-control to wrangle her emotions. She focused on her breathing. One in, two out. One in, two out. Her heart rate slowed. Still, she gripped Logan's arm as if he might disappear.

He leaned in close to her ear. "Are you hurt?"

"No." She leaned in close to whisper in his ear. "He's near the Jeep. I pepper sprayed him. Got some in my eyes, too, but the pain is fading."

He gently touched her face, swiping the tears from her cheeks. "I have to go after him."

"I'm coming. He could be anywhere in these woods, and I'm not staying here by myself."

Logan hesitated and then nodded. "Keep your hand on my belt."

She did as he asked. They crept through the woods back toward the road. Shivers overtook her body, whether from the fear or from the icy wind, Willow couldn't tell. Logan's back was rigid. He kept his gun at the ready and his gaze never stopped roaming.

A break in the trees appeared, revealing the road and the Jeep. Willow inhaled sharply.

The gunman was gone.

Sunshine streamed through the half-closed blinds on the windows, casting patterns on the carpet. Willow rolled over and checked the time. Ten in the morning. She hadn't slept last night, falling asleep only after daybreak. Exhaustion threatened to pull her back into a dreamless state, but she fought against it. Sleeping the day away wouldn't solve her problems.

She swung her legs over the bed. Every movement made her body hurt. Scrapes on her feet—earned after she'd run through the woods barefoot—rubbed against the plush carpet as she headed for the bathroom. The pain was a reminder of what she'd endured. A glance in the bathroom mirror confirmed Willow looked as bad as she felt. Her blonde hair was tousled from a restless night, mascara smeared on her face like a set of double black eyes.

She took a quick shower and then pulled on a pair of jeans and a soft T-shirt. The scent of coffee seeped through her closed bedroom door and practically called her name. Willow's stomach rumbled. She hadn't eaten since lunch yesterday. It was late for breakfast, but she had a craving for pancakes with maple syrup. It was the best comfort food.

Willow stopped short after opening her bedroom door. Connor lay in the hallway, just over the threshold. The German shepherd lifted himself off the carpet and came to sniff her hand. She patted his head. "Were you keeping guard, boy?"

He gave her wrist a lick in response. It touched her immensely that Jason had left his dog to watch over her. Logan's friends were thoughtful and honorable. Their quick thinking last night had aided several party guests after the smoke bombs created panic and mass confusion. Thankfully, no one had been seriously injured. Logan's calf had required six stitches, but he would make a full recovery. Willow thanked God repeatedly for protecting them.

"Come on, Connor. Let's go make some pancakes."

The dog trotted down the hall behind her toward the kitchen. Mia was seated at the table, school books spread open in front of her, a laptop at her elbow. Her dark hair was pulled into a ponytail. She'd paired combat boots with cropped jeans and another flannel shirt. Her eyeliner was winged, but she'd ditched the dark lipstick for a clear gloss.

"Morning, Mia." Willow gave the teen a bright smile before beelining for the coffee pot. Through the window, in the backyard, she spotted Logan speaking with Jason and Kyle near the barbecue. They were probably talking about the attack last night. Willow didn't have the strength to deal with that at the moment. First coffee and pancakes.

Connor stood next to the back door, so she let him into the yard. He raced straight for his owner. The joy on Jason's face as he greeted his dog made Willow smile. Maybe when this was over, she'd get a dog. It'd only been a few days, but she'd grown attached to the German shepherd.

Logan glanced up and caught her eye through the glass pane. Just a simple look, but she felt every one of her nerve endings take notice. The memory of their passionate kiss last night played in her mind. Willow nearly touched her lips before catching herself. Instead, she gave a wave before turning back to Mia. "I know it's a bit late for breakfast, but I'm going to make some pancakes. Would you like some?"

Mia's expression brightened. "I'd love some." She glanced at her watch. "I only have about twenty minutes before my grandmother is picking me up to take me to the youth center though."

"Then you get the first batch."

Willow quickly pulled the ingredients out of the pantry and set them on the counter. She eyed her recipe and then the group of men outside. She'd need to double it, easily. The guys probably had breakfast already, but they loved to eat.

Mia came to join her, leaning against the island. "Have you heard from Josie lately? I called and texted her yesterday and she didn't answer." She twirled a strand of hair between her fingers. "You don't think she could be mad at me, do you? I apologized about the break-in and we've hung out several times since then. She seemed fine when I saw her two days ago, but…"

"I wouldn't worry." Willow measured flour into a mixing bowl. "Josie has a habit of ignoring her phone and staying off social media when she's composing new songs. Something about immersing herself in the music. I've had trouble reaching her from time-to-time myself. She usually pops back up a day or two later."

Relief flickered across Mia's features. "That makes sense. She mentioned something about a new chord being stuck in her head."

Willow flipped on the stove. "What do you think of the youth center?"

"I like it. The kids there are cool." Mia was quiet for a long moment. "Can I ask you a personal question?"

"You can ask me anything you want." She poured pancake batter onto the hot griddle.

"How long did it take after losing your parents for things to feel normal?"

Willow's chest clenched at the pain vibrating through Mia's voice. She sensed the teen was on the verge of turning a corner and what happened in this conversation would have an impact. Being honest was essential, but so was being hopeful.

She flipped the pancakes, keeping her attention on the cooking because it would make this difficult conversation easier for Mia. "The death of my parents was a demarcation line in my life. It changed me forever. There was no way to go back to the way things were before, because I was different." Willow contemplated her next words. "Losing your parents has changed you, Mia, and you'll never go back to the person you used to be. But that doesn't mean you can't be happy. It took a while for me to understand, but the best way to honor my parents and the love they gave me was to become the best version of myself."

Mia studied the twisting veins in the marble countertop. "I have all these emotions about their deaths. I've been angry with everyone."

"You've gone through something very difficult. It's normal to need time to process it." Willow plated some pancakes and pushed them toward Mia. "And you'll always miss your parents. That won't change. But the pain will fade to a dull ache." She retrieved the butter and syrup, placing them on the island. "You also have people in your life who love you. Your uncle and grandparents. They can't read your mind, so you have to talk to them about what you're feeling. Let them, and God, help with your grief."

Mia's nose wrinkled. "That's not easy."

Willow chuckled. "I know." She poured more batter onto the griddle. "There's one more piece of advice I can give you. Prayer makes things better. Always. Whatever questions you have, whatever feelings you're going through, share them with Him. You may be surprised about how much better you feel afterward."

The doorbell rang. Mia shoved the last bite of pancake into her mouth. "That's my grandmother."

The next few minutes were a flurry of activity as Mia packed up her bag and said goodbye to Logan. Then she surprised Willow by hugging her. "Thanks for the talk."

"Anytime, Mia."

The teen bounced down the porch steps to the car. Willow felt Logan's gaze on her, but he didn't say anything until they were back inside the kitchen. "What did you and Mia discuss?"

"Her parents. Faith." She placed a stack of pancakes on the island. "I hope you don't mind."

"Not at all. In fact, I told her you were a good person to talk to." He was silent for a beat. "I wish Mia felt comfortable discussing things with me."

"She will." Willow hesitated, trying to figure out the right way to phrase her next words. "Vulnerability isn't easy. Mia is a lot like you. She's built a wall to protect herself, and it'll take time to get through those defenses. Just be patient."

Logan's mouth twitched. "Are you saying that I'm expecting too much?"

She held up two fingers close together. "Maybe just a little." Willow dropped her hand. "One observation. When Mia does speak to you, share your own fears and worries with her. It'll help."

He winced. "I'm not good at that."

"I understand, but Mia needs to feel like she's not alone."

Logan nodded. "It seems like she's moving in the right direction. Is that safe to say?"

"I think so. She's a smart, lovely young woman." Willow smiled. "I mean, don't get me wrong. She's still a teenager. Mia's going to push your buttons, but I think she'll do less of it now."

He laughed. "That's a bargain I can live with." Logan's smile faded and he reached for Willow's hand. "There's something we need to discuss. The sooner, the better."

Her muscles stiffened. "It's about last night, isn't it?"

He nodded. "I'm sorry to tell you this, Willow, but I think your ex might be involved."

FOURTEEN

Rain sprinkled against the windshield when Logan pulled into the parking lot of Nelson's Diner. Crooked blinds hung in the windows and the building desperately needed a fresh coat of paint. A mix of onions and fresh fries fragranced the air. There were only a few other cars in the lot. None of them were Mike's sports car. He wasn't here yet.

Logan shoved the Jeep into park. "Are you sure about doing this? It's not too late to call the meeting off."

"Yes, I'm sure." Willow's expression was hard and determined. "I'm done with sitting on the sidelines. You were shot last night. My bodyguard is dead. Things are out of control. I need to know if Mike is involved."

He wasn't convinced this was the right move, but interviewing Mike could break the case wide open. Logan killed the engine. "Okay. Let's do this."

"Hold on." Willow pushed a button on her cell phone and then lifted it to her ear. The sound of the line ringing filtered from the speaker, then Josie's voice came on, spouting a standard greeting and a request for the person to leave a message. Willow took a deep breath. "Hey, Josie, it's me. Give me a call or shoot me a text when you get this and let me know you're okay. Thanks, bye."

She hung up, a worried look etched across her features.

Logan frowned. "What's going on with Josie?"

"Nothing. I'm being a worrywart." Willow shoved her cell in her purse. "Mia mentioned she couldn't reach Josie yesterday. I sent her a text earlier, and she didn't reply to me either. Josie ignores her phone when she's composing. I'm sure she's just working on a new song, but with everything going on, it would be nice to have confirmation."

"I can send someone to Josie's house to check on her."

Willow drummed her nails against the door handle. "Tomorrow. Let's give her a bit longer to reply. Like I said, this isn't unusual for her." She gave him a wry smile. "Josie accuses me of being a mama bear as it is. I don't want to give her another thing to tease me about."

"You care about her. Nothing wrong with that."

"I know. Secretly, I think Josie likes it. She doesn't have a relationship with her father and her mom is dead. We spend most of our holidays together. She's family to me." Willow's gaze drifted toward the diner beyond the rain speckled windshield. Her nose wrinkled. "I'm not one to judge a book by its cover, but this place could use a bit of sprucing up."

Logan laughed, reaching for the umbrella tucked in the pocket behind Willow's seat. "It's rustic."

"That's one way of putting it."

He shook his head, still laughing, and exited the vehicle before circling around to open her door. The stitches in his calf pulled with every step, but the pain was manageable.

Willow slipped her hand into his as she used the sideboard to step down. Warmth flowed from the point of contact, up Logan's arm, and into his chest. He took a chance and interlaced their fingers. Willow smiled up at him in response. His heart skipped a beat.

They hadn't spoken about the kiss or what it meant yet. Logan wasn't in a hurry. Willow was going through a stressful time, and he didn't want to rock the boat between them. Whatever was happening would be sorted out in time. The priority had to be finding whoever was behind these attacks.

A bell hung over the door jingled as they entered the restaurant.

Harriet, an apron wrapped around her ample waist, hurried around the front counter to embrace Logan in a hug. "I'm so glad you're here. And in one piece. I was worried sick after I heard about what happened last night." She pulled back, her cheeks plumping with the effort of her smile as her gaze fell on Willow. "Hello, dear. You must be Willow. It's so nice to meet you. I've heard such wonderful things about you from Addison and the other ladies."

Willow blushed. "It's nice to meet you, too, ma'am. Addison was kind enough to bring some of your pies over to my house the other night. They were outstanding."

Harriet beamed. "That's sweet of you to say. Which was your favorite, if you don't mind me asking?"

"It's hard to pick just one, but if I was forced to choose, it'd be the peach. Warmed up with a little vanilla ice cream." Willow lifted her fingers to her mouth and kissed them. "A little slice of heaven."

"Well, you're in luck because I just happened to have a

fresh peach pie in the oven." Harriet winked at Logan. "Don't think I forgot about you. I've saved a piece of lemon meringue in the back. It's got your name on it."

Lemon meringue was his favorite. Harriet never forgot to keep it on hand for Logan. He slung an arm over her shoulders as she escorted them to a table. "You're the best, Harriet."

"I know." She lightly whacked him with the menus. "And don't you forget it, son."

"No, ma'am."

Harriet stopped in front of a booth next to the window overlooking the parking lot. Logan lifted his hand to wave at Nelson, visible in the kitchen through a cutout behind a counter lined with barstools, before moving aside so Willow could sit first. Then he slid in next to her. Their positions would force Mike to sit across from them, which would make studying his body language a lot easier.

Harriet took their drink orders and then bustled off to another table. Logan pursued the menu, but nothing was appealing. He was too tense to eat. From the way Willow kept glancing at the parking lot, she was feeling the same. Logan placed a hand over hers. "Maybe we should order food after we finish talking to Mike."

She nodded and then jutted her chin toward the window. "There he is now."

Logan's gaze shot to the parking lot. Mike was shutting the driver's side door on his black Porsche. He was dressed in slacks and a Polo shirt, a sweater thrown over his shoulders and knotted at the base of his neck. It looked like he'd just come from a golf course or the country club.

Willow's muscles tensed as Mike crossed the parking lot

and entered the diner. Logan squeezed her hand reassuringly. She met his gaze for half a heartbeat before a mask slipped over her pretty features, hiding her emotions.

Logan released her hand and rose to greet Mike.

Willow nodded as her ex slid into the booth. "Thanks for taking the time to meet with us."

"Of course." Mike flashed her a smile. "I'm glad you called. Scott's campaign isn't going well, and I'd like to do everything I can to turn the situation around."

"It's interesting you say that. I've looked at his latest poll numbers and the race isn't even close. Uncle Scott is ten points ahead and there are only three weeks until Election Day." Willow arched her brows. "What makes you think his campaign isn't going well?"

"The media coverage right now is brutal. The only questions the reporters are asking him are about the attacks. That's an issue. If Scott doesn't talk about the problems his constituents are facing, then they're going to think he doesn't care about them." Mike leaned forward, as if he was about to pounce on Willow. "We need to get ahead of this story. If you do one interview, I think that can answer most of the questions and the media will stop asking Scott."

Logan willed himself to keep his posture relaxed. Everything about Mike sent off his internal senses, honed from over a decade tangling with tangos half a world away. He didn't trust the preppy poser farther than he could throw him. Nor did he like the way Mike was looking at Willow. As though she was a tool he could use for his own purposes.

She'd been right last night. Mike's only interest was himself.

Willow was quiet for a beat. "Even if I were to agree

with you, Mike, there's a bigger problem at hand. The attacks against me aren't over. Last night was proof of that."

Mike pinched the bridge of his nose and groaned. "The party was a disaster. Another event like that and Scott can kiss this election goodbye." He dropped his hand. "The police don't have any idea who is behind this?"

"They have two theories. Either someone wants my uncle to drop out of the campaign and will do anything possible to make that happen, or the attacker has a personal vendetta against my family." Willow folded her hands over the table. "Why are you here, Mike?"

His brow creased. "Kathryn needs help managing the last weeks of this campaign and made me an offer I couldn't refuse. What does that have to do with the attacks against you?"

"It's an interesting coincidence that you showed up right after the attacks against Willow started." Logan kept his gaze locked on the man sitting across the table. "And I don't believe in coincidences."

Mike's cordial expression faded. He glared at Logan. "I don't take kindly to being accused of a crime. You need to be very careful about what comes out of your mouth next."

Logan nearly laughed. The little peon didn't scare him. Mike wasn't someone who would ever fight his own battles. He was a coward, through and through. His horrible treatment of Willow five years ago when they were dating was proof of his character.

Mike swung his gaze back toward Willow. "I know things didn't end well with us, but I would never purposefully hurt you. Never."

What a load of baloney. Logan was done with the innocent act. "Two years ago, your younger brother, Samuel, was convicted of involuntary manslaughter after he plowed into a woman while driving drunk. It was his third DUI. Scott Buchanan was the prosecuting attorney. You begged him to send your brother to a rehab program after the guilty verdict came back. He refused. Instead, Scott recommended the maximum sentence to the judge. Samuel was sent to prison for twenty years. Two weeks later, he died in a violent fight among inmates." Logan pinned the other man with his gaze. "Maybe you're looking to get revenge against Scott for your brother's death."

"By killing Willow?" Mike scoffed. "That's a stretch. If I wanted to hurt Scott, I would take a more direct approach. Smear him in the media, for starters."

"Why would you work on Scott's campaign at all? Given your history with the Buchanan family, it seems like a strange career move."

"Because Scott can't be bought, which is more than I can say for Senator Randall. That man is a nightmare. I'm sure you've heard about his under-the-table dealings." He leaned forward. "What happened with my brother was tragic, but I never blamed Scott. Samuel made a series of bad decisions and ended up dead as a result."

Mike sounded genuine, but the man was a con artist. He'd strung Willow along for months and pretended to be in love with her. He knew how to sell a lie. Something about this didn't add up.

Logan tilted his head. "You expect us to believe that you want to work for Scott's campaign because he's the honest candidate?"

"I don't care what you believe. I don't need to explain myself to you."

"Are you trying to kill me, Mike?" Willow's question came out low to keep anyone from overhearing, but it was loud enough to carry across the booth. Her chin was jutted up, her gaze fixed on her ex.

"No. It's absolutely preposterous that you would think so." Mike rose from the booth, adjusting the sweater on his shoulders with angry gestures. "Let me give you a bit of advice, Willow. If you're searching for suspects, you should look at those closest to you."

She blinked. "What does that mean?"

"Your trust fund. If I remember correctly, it doesn't fully pay out until you're forty. That makes you worth a lot of money." Mike arched his brow. "Enough for someone to kill for."

FIFTEEN

Willow tossed her calculator down on the desk before folding her arms and dropping her head into them. Thirty cancellations for the Blessed Heart gala had come in since yesterday. Five more this morning. She'd spent the last hour crunching the numbers, but even if she reduced the catering order, the youth center was still in the red. There was no way to make up for the loss.

She felt rather than heard Logan come up behind her. He placed his hands on her shoulders and kneaded the knotted muscles. Willow appreciated that he didn't offer empty platitudes.

She wanted to cry. The attacks had been harrowing and emotionally draining on their own. Now, they were preventing her from fundraising the money they'd need for the outdoor recreational center. Not that she could blame people. After what happened at Scott's birthday party, it made sense to steer clear of anything associated with her.

"Is there anything I can do?" Logan asked.

Willow lifted her head. "No. I've publicly announced

that I won't be attending the gala, and spoken personally with some of the bigger donors, but it hasn't made a dent. They're scared. I don't blame them."

She rose from her chair and turned to look out the window. An enthusiastic baseball game was underway between the youth center and members of the fire department. Various food trucks were stationed in the parking lot, festive balloons and signs pointing to different activities, like the face-painting station. Stands specifically set up for the event were mostly empty. They should've been filled with spectators. All of it, except for the volunteers playing the baseball team, cost money.

This event would also be a financial loss. In a week, her entire life had been turned upside down.

Why, God? Why?

"I don't know where to go from here." Willow blew out a breath. "Until my attacker is caught, everything is in limbo. The constant fear and worry about what he might do next is making it difficult to think. Maybe I should've taken my uncle's advice and gone to a safe house."

"Hindsight is always 20/20. You didn't know back then things would get so bad. No one did."

No. She hadn't. Willow crossed her arms over her chest as a shiver raced down her spine. "I can't stop thinking about what Mike said yesterday about my trust fund."

"It's been on my mind too. I'm glad you brought it up." Logan leaned against the desk. "I didn't understand his accusation because you told me a few days ago that you'd used your trust fund to build the youth center."

"I did. When the trust was created, my parents gave instructions for the payments to happen throughout my life.

One paid for my college, the other my masters. I received a significant sum when I was twenty-five, which is what I used to create Blessed Hearts. The final and last payment is the largest. I will receive it when I'm forty." She chewed on the inside of her cheek. "Uncle Scott is the trustee, which means he has access and control of the money in the fund."

Understanding dawned in Logan's expression. "So he could use it to pay a ransom, let's say."

"In theory, yes. Although knowledge of the trust fund and its amount is a closely guarded secret. There are only a handful of people who know about it." Heat infused her cheeks. "Mike overheard Uncle Scott and me speaking about it once, which is how he's aware of its existence. I was furious when I found out. The conversation was private."

"When you say only a handful of people know about it..."

"Uncle Scott, Kathryn. A few members of our extended family. Our lawyers and accountants."

"Can I ask how much money is in your trust fund?"

Willow hesitated. "Fifteen million dollars."

He whistled. "That's a chunk of change." Logan was quiet for a long moment. "The attacker attempted to kidnap you from Scott's birthday party. You're thinking money could be the motive?"

"I don't know. We've been so fixated on the idea that these threats are connected to Uncle Scott's campaign, or some kind of vendetta against the family, it never occurred to me to consider ransom as a motive." Willow didn't want to voice the next part. It was heinous, but keeping it inside wasn't helping. "Kathryn and Uncle Scott have a prenuptial agreement. She gets some money if they divorce, but it's not significant. We don't have the best relationship, and after Mike's accusation last night…"

"You're wondering if Kathryn told him something."

"I hate to think so, but they seemed friendly with each other in the library before we walked in." Willow rubbed her forehead. "Tell me this is a wild theory that makes no sense."

"No theory outside of aliens is too wild at this point. We don't have a lot of physical evidence to go on." Logan crossed his arms over his chest. "However, the attacker's been sending stalking photographs to Scott and terrorizing text messages to you. The car bombing. None of that fits with a normal kidnapping for ransom."

"True. It's part of the reason I didn't think of it earlier."

He held up a hand. "Hold on. Let's not dismiss this idea too fast. What happens to the money in the trust if you're killed?"

"Uncle Scott inherits it. But he would never hurt me, not in a million years."

"Understood. But who inherits if he dies?"

Willow stilled, her body growing cold. "Kathryn." Her mind whirled. "But she would have to kill us both. Wouldn't that look suspicious?"

"Not if the police believe your family has been targeted by someone seeking a vendetta. First you die tragically, then your uncle." Logan lifted one shoulder. "It fits with the evidence. Is there any indication that your uncle and Kathryn are having trouble in their marriage? Any sign she wants out of the relationship?"

"Not that I've seen. Although both Uncle Scott and Kathryn are private people. They've never spoken about marriage troubles to me." Willow felt a wave of guilt and shame. Was she really accusing Kathryn of trying to kill her? It was disturbing. "I hate this. I don't want to be suspicious of everyone I know, especially people in my family. It feels like Mike is inside my head all over again, manipulating me. He may have thrown out that accusation to distract us from his own involvement."

"It's possible. I don't trust that guy one iota. Senator Randall is still high on my suspect list as well." Logan pushed off from the desk and came to stand next to her. "Things always look bleak when you're in the storm, but hold on. We'll sort this out."

His tone was gentle and kind. Willow reached for him, burying her face in his broad chest, inhaling the scent of his laundry soap and aftershave. Logan's hand dipped into her hair, his fingers tangling with the strands. His embrace was comforting. The sounds of the ball striking against the bat, followed by a round of cheers filtered through the closed window.

Willow's muscles relaxed. "I'm glad you're here."

"So I am." He kissed the crown of her head before resting his cheek against it.

The embrace was both intimate and loving. Her feelings for Logan were deepening with every moment she spent in his presence. They hadn't discussed the kiss, but she sensed something had shifted between them. Barriers had broken down on both sides.

Willow was tempted to ask what it all meant, but with the threats hanging over her head, it didn't feel like the right time. There was too much at risk. Logan cared for her. That much was obvious. But what if he didn't want a relationship? The rejection would sting. It was better to leave things as they were between them for the moment.

She lifted her head and was about to back out of Logan's arms when their gazes caught. The look in his eyes held her captive. Willow's breath hitched as he leaned forward. Without thinking, she met him halfway. The world tilted on its axis as their lips met. Logan drew her closer.

This kiss differed from their first. The one in her uncle's library had been passionate and fevered, born from unspoken desire and a dangerous situation. This… this was gentle and seductive. Heady enough to make Willow's head spin and her knees weak. She clung to his broad shoulders, riding the wave of emotions tumbling inside her as the world narrowed to the intensity of their embrace. She never wanted it to end.

Logan drew back, resting his forehead against hers. His breathing was rapid, and under Willow's palm resting on his chest, his heart thundered. She'd done that to him. Unsettled this rough and hardened soldier. It sent a thrill through her to realize the passion between them was shared. Where it would go, she didn't know. It didn't matter. Right now, she was content to be present in the moment with him.

His phone rang. Logan groaned. "I have to answer that."

He brushed another kiss across Willow's mouth before releasing her. Then he dug the cell out of his pocket. "Keller."

In an instant, his mood shifted. Logan's muscles tensed as he listened to whoever was on the other line. "We'll be right there."

Fear doused Willow like a bucket of cold water. She grabbed his arm. "What is it?"

"It's Josie." Logan's expression darkened with worry. "Tucker went to do a wellness check on her this morning, but she's not answering the door. Neighbors haven't seen her in a few days, which as you pointed out, is normal when she's composing music. Her car is in the garage and the home is locked up tight. Normally, Tucker wouldn't worry since Josie is an adult, but he's been ringing the bell and pounding on the door for the last five minutes with no response. As a police officer, he can't enter the house without a sign of imminent danger. Since you have a key—"

"I can go inside." Willow grabbed her purse. "Let's go."

The drive to Josie's house took less than fifteen minutes. Willow prayed the young woman was simply lost in a creative zone, but she had a horrible feeling that something was wrong.

Logan parked his Jeep behind Tucker's patrol car. Willow got out of the vehicle, Josie's house keys already in her hand. She climbed the walkway, Logan hot on her heels.

Tucker, in uniform, stood on the front porch. His red hair shone in the sunlight. "Thanks for coming so quickly. Since I'm not legally allowed to enter the house, I have to stay here."

Willow nodded and slid the key in the lock. The door popped open easily. It swung wide, revealing a dim entryway and the living room beyond. All the blinds in the house were drawn tight.

The pit of unease in Willow's stomach grew. "Josie, are you here? It's Willow."

Silence was the only response. She stepped over the threshold, pulse racing. "Josie, it's Willow."

Logan stopped her with a hand on her arm. "Let me go in first."

He'd already pulled his weapon, which only spiked her pulse. A fresh wave of adrenaline coursed through her veins. She considered arguing for a moment—after all, they were invading Josie's personal space—but wisdom held her tongue. Something about this wasn't right. Willow knew it.

She stepped to the side so he could pass in front of her. Logan moved deeper into the house on measured steps. Nothing appeared disturbed in the kitchen. The counter was wiped clean, and the sink was devoid of dirty plates. The mudroom contained a washer and dryer, a few pairs of shoes lined up underneath a bench next to the door leading to the backyard. Josie's SUV sat in the garage.

They backtracked into the living room. The drawn blinds concerned Willow. Josie loved sunshine almost as much as her daily exercise. It was nearly noon. She would never keep her shades closed at this late hour. "Josie, it's Willow and Logan. Are you here?"

A faint thumping echoed down the hall. Willow's heart skipped a beat. She followed closely behind Logan as he hastened toward the first bedroom. A light streamed from underneath the closed door. The thumping continued at an irregular rate. Willow couldn't make heads or tails of it.

Logan pushed the door open. She rounded the corner and gasped.

Josie lay in a pool of blood at the base of her piano bench. She'd been beaten, the room ransacked. One hand weakly beat against the floor wood, which had been the thumping Willow heard. The other hand clutched at a seeping wound along her abdomen.

Logan raced to the young woman's side. "Willow, have Tucker call EMS and grab the medic kit from the back of my Jeep."

His words were clipped, his tone urgent. She turned to do his bidding. Something scrawled across the wall halted her forward momentum for half a heartbeat.

A message written in Josie's blood.

I'm going to make you pay.

SIXTEEN

Logan paced the length of the hospital emergency room. He'd washed Josie's blood off his hands, but nothing could remove the stains on his clothes. Along with being beaten, the young woman had been stabbed. She'd been alive when the doctors whisked her into surgery. Barely.

Now they had to wait. And pray.

The doors leading to the emergency room swished open and Tucker emerged. His expression was grim. Willow rose from a chair, her hand going to her throat. Logan closed the distance between them, wrapping an arm around her waist, bracing himself for whatever news was coming.

Tucker stopped in front of them. "Josie made it through surgery and is in the ICU. It's going to be touch-and-go for a while, but she's young and strong. The doctors believe she'll make a full recovery. Her aunt is with her now and will stay through the night."

"Thank God." Willow sagged against Logan. Tears flooded her eyes and dripped onto her cheeks. She swiped them away with a shaky hand. "Was she able to identify her attacker?"

"No." Tucker glanced around the immediate area, but their section was devoid of people. "All Josie could tell me was that he wore a ski mask. From what I could gather, she was working on her music late last night when a large man appeared in the doorway. He viciously attacked her and then left."

Willow shuddered. "She lay there all night and morning, bleeding out, alone and afraid."

Rage coursed through Logan's veins, but he tamped it down. The emotion wouldn't help him. "The attack on Josie has to be connected to Willow."

"I agree." Tucker tilted his head toward a hallway on their left. "Come on. I called the guys and they're waiting for us in a break room. We can discuss the case there."

They traipsed past the front desk and down several empty corridors to a quiet break room on the second floor. It had a circular table, a small kitchenette, and a few couches arranged in front of a television. The fridge was dented and had seen better days. The space smelled of floor cleaner and fresh coffee.

Kyle, Nathan, Walker, and Jason greeted Willow warmly before sharing brotherly hugs with Logan. Connor's wet nose nudged his hand. Logan patted the German shepherd affectionately. Boxes etched with the Nelson's Diner logo rested on the scratched table, along with plastic silverware and paper plates.

Nathan handed Logan a takeaway mug filled to the brim with steaming coffee. "Harriet sends her love."

He sipped the precious brew and reminded himself to

bring a bouquet of roses to Harriet. The woman was a treasure.

Beside him, Willow took a sip of her own coffee and hummed with approval. She eyed the boxes on the table. "Please tell me those contain pie."

"They do." Nathan crowed with happiness. He tossed his cowboy hat on the couch nearby. "Let's eat first. I can't think on an empty stomach."

"You can't think with a full stomach," Kyle teased his cousin.

The two men got into a ribbing war that the others were quickly pulled into. Willow laughed several times, joining in on the fun. It was obvious she adored his friends. And her ability to find stolen moments of joy even with everything going on was a testament to the strength of her character. She was amazing.

The memory of their stolen kisses flooded Logan's mind. He was definitely falling for the gorgeous blonde, but there was so much uncertainty about the future of their relationship. For starters, there was Mia to consider. She would always be Logan's priority. Willow was great with teens. She'd dedicated her life to helping them, but that didn't mean she wanted to be a part of raising one 24-7.

And although Mia had seemed fine with the idea of Logan and Willow dating, that could shift once real life set in. Teens were notorious for changing their minds. Mia was just starting to get back on the right track. Did Logan really want to shake things up at home?

It was a lot to consider, and right now, he didn't have the mental bandwidth to tackle the issues.

Once everyone had their fill of pie, Logan clapped his

hands together to halt the conversation. The air in the room immediately shifted as everyone fixed their gaze on him. He shoved his empty plate to the side. "Let's get down to business. Tucker, what can you tell us about the attack on Josie?"

"The intruder came in through a broken bedroom window and left the same way. He viciously beat Josie before stabbing her twice." Tucker didn't mince words, but his voice vibrated with suppressed anger. "According to Josie, she played dead while he wrote the message in blood on her wall. That move likely saved her life."

Logan's jaw clenched as his imagination took hold. Thinking about what Josie had gone through wouldn't find her attacker. He needed to focus. "Josie's assailant is likely the same one attempting to kill Willow. Leaving his victim alive was a sloppy move."

"Agreed, but this guy hasn't had much success in killing Willow either. He's angry, and it's causing him to make mistakes. Unfortunately, Josie doesn't have security cameras in her house. Officers are asking the neighbors, but at the moment, we don't even have a description of the assailant." He practically growled with frustration. "He's a ghost."

"I might be able to help." Kyle rubbed his bloodshot eyes. "I've been watching security video of Scott's birthday party for days trying to spot when the smoke bombs were placed. It wasn't easy to identify one individual because there were three hundred people in and out of the house in the days leading up to the party."

"Three hundred?" Walker's mouth dropped open. "What were they doing?"

"Flowers, lights, catering, cleaning crew... the list goes

on and on. Putting on a party like that is a huge production. Anyway, one guy on the staff stuck out. He used a fake name and a fake address when applying for a temporary position with the party planner." Kyle tapped on his phone and set it on the table. "Anyone recognize him?"

The image was grainy. The man was average looking with a receding hairline, thick brows, and a thin mouth. He could've been anywhere from thirty to fifty. The kind of guy that blended into the wallpaper. Still, recognition zipped through Logan. "He worked the coat check at Scott's house on the night of the party."

Willow nodded. "Yes, you're right. Do you know his real name?"

"Devon James. Originally from Wisconsin. Thirty-four. Former Army Ranger. He was dishonorably discharged after being convicted of beating his wife badly enough to put her in the hospital. After that, Devon spent time building an extensive criminal record. Breaking and entering, robbery, etc. Spent ten years in prison for murdering his second wife while drunk. Got out and was arrested a year later on a murder-for-hire charge here in Texas. Devon was supposed to kill a wealthy doctor's wife. Doctor was having an affair with his mistress and wanted to avoid a lengthy divorce. Case was dropped because there wasn't enough evidence. Devon disappeared off the grid after that."

Dread touched the back of Logan's neck, making the hair at his nape stand on end. "If Devon was willing to take a murder-for-hire job once, maybe he'd do it again."

"That's what I'm thinking. I've done all I can to cross-reference him to anyone in your family and came up empty-handed." Nathan glanced at Willow. "Other than the party, have you ever seen him before?"

"No."

"Then I think it's safe to conclude Devon is working for someone else. The question is who?"

"You haven't been able to connect Devon to any of our suspects? Senator Randall, Mike, or Kathryn."

"Nope. But that doesn't mean much. He could be using a burner phone while communicating with the mastermind of this operation. People hire hitmen online. I'll continue to dig, though. There may be a connection that's buried deep."

Jason leaned forward. "Walker and I have been tracking down everyone who's ever accused Senator Randall of wrongdoing. No one will talk to us, other than the reporter, Ken Watson. He's agreed to give a statement to Chief Garcia, but it's not evidence to launch an investigation into the senator. Randall never directly threatened him."

"Reporters often make enemies," Tucker pointed out. "Are we sure the threats can be connected to Senator Randall?"

Jason frowned. The movement stretched the scar on the side of his face. "No, but people are scared of Randall."

"Very scared," Nathan added. The cowboy hat had left an impression in his hair and he had a smudge of cherry pie on the corner of his mouth. "Several people warned me against investigating him, but wouldn't explain why."

"Unfortunately, that's not enough to go on. We need hard evidence linking him to Devon or the threats against Willow." Logan shifted his gaze to Kyle. "Were you able to trace the email sent to Scott? The one with the photographs of Willow in a sniper's crosshairs."

"I'm working on it, but I need more time." Kyle arched his brows. "I prioritized the surveillance video from the party. The email is next on my list."

"Got it." He turned to Walker. "What did you find out about Mike Jensen?"

"Other than he's a sneaky weasel who can't be trusted? Plenty. For starters, Mike has a reputation for being cutthroat in politics and likes to play dirty. He's romanced about half a dozen wealthy socialites, but none of the relationships stuck. Until recently. He's currently engaged to Senator Randall's niece. The family isn't happy about it and things have become strained."

Willow frowned. "That's strange. Senator Randall isn't known for being kind when it comes to politics. His ads against my uncle are very negative. Why wouldn't he want Mike working for his campaign?"

"Apparently, there was a fight between the two men at a family gathering shortly after Mike started dating the senator's niece. I don't know the details, but whatever transpired destroyed any chance they had of working together."

"I could see that," Logan said. "Mike's arrogant. Randall doesn't strike me as someone who would tolerate anyone stealing his spotlight. Were you able to uncover anything about Mike's feelings toward Scott after his brother died?"

"I talked to a couple of ex-girlfriends. They said Mike was quiet about his brother's death. Never discussed it, even after he went to the funeral, although they all confirmed Mike and Samuel were close." Walker shrugged his wide shoulders. "If he's harboring a grudge against Scott, he didn't say so to anyone."

Logan mulled that bit of information over. Mike was

cunning enough to play the long game. It was hard to believe Mike didn't experience any grief after Samuel's passing. Pain could morph into vengeance easily. "I can't shake the feeling that Mike's wrapped up in this somehow. He came to work for Scott's campaign. That can't be a coincidence."

"I confirmed that Kathryn offered him the job, Mike didn't seek her out." Walker ran a hand through his close-cropped hair. "He also has a bone to pick with Senator Randall. There may be nothing more to it."

His friend had a point. Logan decided to let it go for now. He turned to Jason. "Were you able to gather any information on Kathryn's finances?"

"She doesn't have much in her name. She inherited some old warehouses on the outskirts of town from a maternal grandmother, but hasn't done anything with them. Before marrying Scott, she was a news reporter, but the pay wasn't much. She buys designer clothes and her monthly shoe allowance is more than the average person makes all year. My wife Addison knows some women in Kathryn's social circle and quietly made inquiries." Jason rubbed the scar alongside his cheek absently as he consulted his notes. "Kathryn's friends consider her generous. She's known for throwing lavish parties and picking up the tab for lunch. They also described her as wickedly smart and a hard worker. Everyone is under the impression Scott's senatorial campaign wouldn't have been a success without her at the helm."

"Any hint of problems between her and Scott?"

"A few rumblings, but nothing concrete."

Logan glanced at Willow. "I think it's time we speak to

Kathryn. I'd like to know why she offered Mike the job in the first place, especially since she knew about the falling out you had with him. She also planned Scott's birthday party. If Devon is secretly working for her, it would've been a simple matter of connecting him with the catering company."

Willow hesitated and then nodded. "We have to tread lightly. There's no evidence she's involved in any of this."

"Understood."

She was right. They didn't have any evidence of Kathryn's involvement, but Logan couldn't get Willow's fifteen-million-dollar trust fund out of his mind. Most people were killed by someone in their inner circle. The attacks, coupled with the text messages, were overdone for a hitman with no stake in the game. Josie's stabbing, for example, was unnecessary.

Unless the goal was to make it look like Willow was being hunted by someone with a personal vendetta.

Had Kathryn decided she wanted to keep her cushy lifestyle but get out of her marriage?

And was she willing to murder her niece and husband to make it happen?

SEVENTEEN

Willow's stomach twisted into knots as she entered the Buchanan campaign headquarters. The open office space on the ground floor was quiet, since most of the staff had gone home hours ago. Logan shut the door behind them firmly. They'd come up with a plan to extract the necessary information without directly accusing Kathryn of wrongdoing, but that didn't lessen Willow's anxiety. Navigating this conversation wouldn't be easy.

As far as she was concerned, it was farfetched to consider Kathryn a suspect. The woman was demanding and loved money, but that didn't make her a killer. Then again, Willow couldn't rely on her own judgment. Mike had tricked her into believing he was trustworthy at one point too. She'd been wrong about him. It was only reasonable to accept she could be wrong about Kathryn as well.

Willow glanced at the second floor. The lights in her uncle's office were dark—he had a meeting with the governor tonight—but Kathryn's were on. She was working late. Good. Willow hadn't called ahead but taken a chance that Kathryn would still be in the office. For all her faults, she was a hard worker.

"Are you okay?" Logan asked. He placed a hand on the small of Willow's back. "It's not too late to call this off."

"No." She took a deep breath and squared her shoulders. "Asking these questions is the only way to get to the truth. We may not get another opportunity. I want to use surprise as a..." Willow glanced at his profile. "What did you call it again?"

His lips curved into a brief smile. "Tactical advantage."

"Right." Willow focused back on the second floor. "Kathryn doesn't know we suspect her."

"If she's as smart as you say, she will by the time this conversation is done. It's a risk."

"One I'm willing to accept. Catching her off guard is the best way to get the information we need." She took another deep breath, quenching the last of her anxiety. "Let's do this."

Willow climbed the staircase. She paused, misstep, hand on the railing. Shock reverberated through her. "What is *he* doing here?"

Senator Randall was visible through the glass walls of Kathryn's office. He was chatting with her aunt. From the looks on their faces, the conversation was amenable and friendly. Neither noticed Willow and Logan on the stairs.

"It could be nothing," Logan whispered. "Maybe they're discussing a campaign issue."

"Perhaps." She strained to hear the conversation happening inside. Kathryn's office door was open, the indistinct murmur of voices audible, but Willow couldn't make out the words. The tone seemed as pleasant as their expressions indicated.

A dark suspicion touched the back of her neck with an icy finger. Could Kathryn and Senator Randall be working together? If Willow died, her uncle would drop out of the race, which would benefit the senator. Kathryn would gain access to the trust fund. Or was that theory too farfetched to consider? Willow didn't know. And that was the problem.

She continued to climb the stairs to the landing. Kathryn spotted them. A flicker of alarm widened her eyes before she smoothed the emotion away. She must've said something to Senator Randall because he turned. His gaze locked on Willow. The easy smile plastered on his face shifted into something predatory. It took everything inside Willow to cross the threshold into the office.

Kathryn greeted them with a bright smile that was strained at the edges. "Willow, Logan, what a pleasant surprise." She turned back to Senator Randall. "You remember my niece, senator. And this is her boyfriend, Logan Keller."

"Of course." The senator nodded. "I met Logan last week at the car wash fundraiser."

"I hope we're not interrupting." Willow kept her tone polite. The tension in the room was sending off all her internal warning bells.

Kathryn laughed lightly. "Not at all. Senator Randall was just leaving."

"That's right." He picked up his coat from the back of a visitor's chair and slung it over his arm. "Thank you for meeting with me, Kathryn. Have a good night, everyone."

The senator strolled out of the room without a backward glance. Some of the stiffness in Willow's muscles eased. She didn't like Senator Randall at all. The feeling was instinctual and as undeniable as breathing air. From the way Logan watched the other man exit the building, he shared the sentiment.

Willow focused on Kathryn. "What was Senator Randall doing here?"

"Warning me about Mike." She dropped into her leather desk chair and sighed as though the entire weight of the world was on her shoulders. "Mike's engaged to the senator's niece, who has become estranged from her family recently. They don't approve of Mike at all. He's bad news. A liar and master manipulator."

"You won't get any argument from me on those points." Willow was surprised by the direction of the conversation but decided to use it to her advantage. "Did you know Mike's brother, Samuel, was convicted of involuntary manslaughter after driving drunk? He died in prison. Uncle Scott was the prosecuting attorney on the case."

"That I knew about. Mike explained he admired Scott's honesty and integrity." She fiddled with the pearls hanging around her neck. "At the time, I believed Mike. He was upfront about things most people try to hide. He even came clean right away about his relationship with you."

"He knows how to fool people into believing he's honest." Willow's heart softened toward her aunt. Kathryn had dark circles under her eyes and her suit was uncharacteristically wrinkled. She looked exhausted. "I met with him the other day. You should know, he insinuated money was the motive behind the attacks on my life."

"Money?" Kathryn dropped the pearls, her brows creasing in confusion. Her gaze jumped between Willow and Logan. "I don't understand. Who on earth would..." She inhaled sharply and shot to her feet. Anger created a red stain on her cheeks. "Your trust fund."

"Yes. He made it sound like Uncle Scott or you were behind the attacks."

"That's a nasty accusation. One I'm sure he'll leak to the papers the minute I fire him." Kathryn marched to one end of the office and then turned on her heel. "It was a stupid move on my part to hire Mike. You tried to tell me at Scott's birthday party, Willow, and I refused to listen. I was so caught up in winning this election..."

"Mike said the polls can't be trusted, and that Scott is losing ground with his constituents." Logan rested his hands lightly on the back of a visitor's chair. "Is any of that true?"

"It is. We've increased spending on ads to drive focus back to the issues, but that's expensive. The campaign is running out of cash quickly, which feeds into Mike's narrative. People—especially reporters—love a scandal. What better story is there than a senatorial candidate being accused of murdering his own niece for money?"

Willow had to admit there was truth in Kathryn's logic. The media was already in a frenzy over the case as it was. Reporters were constantly calling, seeking a statement from her. If Scott was accused of hiring a hitman to kill Willow... it would be the end of his campaign. The damage to his reputation would be devastating. It didn't even matter if the accusation was true. People often believed lies.

Was this Mike's objective all along? To destroy Scott by

hurting him in every way possible. In her gut, Willow believed her ex was capable of it. He was cunning. It could explain the tidbit of advice he'd given at the diner. Nothing Mike did was altruistic. He was planting the seed of doubt in Willow's mind, hoping it would bloom into family division and suspicion. Which it had.

Logan pulled out his phone and tapped on the screen. "Have you ever seen this man before? His name is Devon James."

Kathryn stepped closer and studied the image. Confusion flickered across her face. "I'm not sure. Something about him looks familiar, but I see so many people these days. Why are you asking?"

"We believe he may be responsible for the attack during Scott's birthday party. He was working the coat check that night."

Horror widened Kathryn's eyes. The reaction appeared genuine, her shock evident as she reached out to grasp the corner of the desk. She focused on Willow. "Why is he doing this?"

"We don't know. Devon was arrested on a murder-for-hire charge years ago. Maybe he's working for someone else." She kept her gaze on her aunt. "Someone like Mike or Senator Randall. Or some other person we haven't identified yet."

That was a terrifying thought. Willow didn't want to imagine an unknown element in this case. Things were difficult enough as they were.

"Devon was in our house... he can be linked to Scott. Or me. It's a weak link, but things can be spun to make it seem more significant. That adds another level of validity to Mike's claims that we're behind the attacks on you, Willow." Kathryn blew out a breath. "Logan, would you mind giving us a moment alone, please?"

He glanced at Willow and she nodded, showing it was all right. Logan touched her arm briefly as he passed by her. The office door closed behind him.

Kathryn sat and gestured for Willow to do the same. Then she clasped her hands together in her lap. "There are some things you need to know, especially if Mike goes to the media and attempts to smear the Buchanan good name." She took an uneasy breath. "Things between your uncle and I have been strained."

"Strained how?"

"The campaign has taken its toll, both emotionally and financially. Mike wasn't the only error in judgment I've made recently. I've poured a lot of money into running this operation." She waved a hand toward the desks on the first floor. "We're not destitute by any stretch of the imagination, but if reporters dig into our finances... it could add fuel to the fire."

Willow's chest tightened. "Did you tell Mike any of this information? About the financial strain? Or your marriage troubles?"

Kathryn hesitated and then nodded. "All of it. I was foolish to trust him. I know better..." Tears filmed her eyes. "Things were a struggle before the campaign. I wanted to help Scott achieve this goal, to show him how much he means to me. When the campaign faltered, I grew desperate. Mike is one of the best strategists in the state. He was charming and knowledgeable. I ignored every red flag, including the way he'd treated you in the past."

She played with the diamond-studded wedding band on her finger. "Scott was furious when he found out I'd hired Mike. He saw it as a betrayal of the family. Of you. We've had some in-depth conversations and I've come to some realizations. I owe you an apology. And not just for hiring Mike." Kathryn licked her lips nervously. "I haven't treated you fairly since coming into the family. Deep down, I've been jealous of the relationship you have with Scott. There are a lot of reasons for that—past childhood hurts and family trauma—that I won't get into now. The important part is that you know I'm sorry."

Surprise vibrated through Willow followed by a wave of longing. She desperately wanted to believe Kathryn had a change of heart. But could it be trusted? The apology seemed genuine, but the timing was suspect. She wasn't sure how to respond.

The death threats were turning Willow into someone she didn't like, constantly suspicious of everyone and their motives.

She decided to go with the truth. "I've always wanted to have a good relationship with you, Kathryn."

Her aunt smiled. "That's a relief to hear. I know things will take time, but I'm committed to doing my part to make things better."

She rose and embraced Willow. The hug was brief, but it was loving.

Guilt and shame tumbled through Willow as she said her goodbye and headed for the stairs. She shoved the feelings aside and focused on all the information Kathryn shared. There was trouble in her marriage and financial difficulty. Willow had caught her flirting with Mike and having a secret meeting with Senator Randall. It all tangled together in her thoughts, mixing with Kathryn's apology.

This meeting was supposed to clarify things.

It had only made them more confusing.

EIGHTEEN

Later that night, Logan swiped a sponge over a dirty dinner plate before loading it into the dishwasher. Country music played from the small radio on the counter. A light rain pattered against the kitchen windows. Rolling thunder in the distance promised more severe weather later, the storm bringing with it more fall temperatures. Halloween was next week.

He cast a sympathetic glance into the backyard. Jason and Walker were on perimeter duty tonight. Neither of them would complain—soldiers rarely did—but Logan had already messaged them both offering fresh coffee and a hot meal. They hadn't taken him up on it. Maybe later.

Logan took a pile of dirty dishes from Mia and set them in the sink. Tonight, she wore black jeans ripped at the knee and a ribbed T-shirt. Her dark hair was braided. She'd exchanged the dark eyeliner and lipstick for a makeup-free face, but the biggest change was in her expression. The permanent scowl was gone. Mia had been pleasant and chatty over dinner. Willow had helped to keep the conversation moving, her gift for talking to teens obvious in her interactions with his niece.

Since the attack at Scott's birthday party, Logan and Mia had been staying at Willow's house. It was the best way to keep both of them safe. The killer, by assaulting Josie, had demonstrated he was determined to hurt Willow in any way possible. That meant anyone close to her was in danger, including Mia.

"Have you decided what you're going to be for Halloween?" Logan dropped another plate in the dishwasher.

"Not yet. Give me that sponge, will ya? I'll wipe the table."

He did as she requested. Mia returned with the dirty sponge, handed it back, and then leaned against the counter. Her gaze drifted to Willow, who was pacing in the living room while speaking to Scott on the phone. "Is Willow going to be okay, Uncle Logan?"

"She's going through a hard time right now, but yes, she'll be all right." Logan was touched by the question. "You're worried about her, huh?"

"Her. And you." Mia's chin trembled. Tears shimmered in her eyes. "The shooting..."

Logan's heart dropped to his feet and then rammed into his throat. He flipped off the sink and quickly wiped his hands before embracing his niece. They'd had a brief conversation about the shooting, but Mia hadn't wanted to talk much. Logan hadn't forced the matter. Maybe that'd been a mistake.

Teenagers. Raising them wasn't for the faint of heart.

Mia backed out of his embrace and swiped at the tears on her cheeks. "Ugh, I hate crying."

"Sometimes it's necessary." He lightly tapped her temple. "I'm many things, but I'm not a mind reader. Let me in on whatever is going on inside that head of yours."

She laughed lightly. "I know. Willow basically told me the same thing the other day." Mia turned her back to the counter and leaned against it, crossing her arms over her chest. "Most of the time, my thoughts and feelings are jumbled. I want you to protect Willow and keep her safe, but I'm scared." Her voice grew soft. "I lost my parents. I don't want to lose you too."

His chest clenched so tightly it was hard to draw in a breath. Logan wanted to reassure Mia, but he couldn't give her false platitudes. His brother and sister-in-law had died driving home from a restaurant. Death could come at any moment. It was a fact of life and one he'd dealt with in combat.

Mia was a fifteen-year-old kid still grieving the loss of her parents and struggling in her faith. She needed to feel safe. Logan didn't know how to give her that. Ultimately, he couldn't. Only God could provide the reassurance she needed.

Please, Lord, help me find the right words.

Logan placed a hand on her arm. "If it was up to me, I'd live to be a hundred years old, but ultimately, the choice isn't mine. It's God's. None of us know how much time we have on this earth. It's a painful thing to realize, but it's also a gift. We have the opportunity to make each day matter. To better ourselves. To serve others. Protecting Willow... it's something I've been trained to do. God has placed me in her life for a reason. I believe he's placed her in our lives for a reason too."

Mia was quiet. Logan let the silence draw out, letting her process his words in her own time.

Finally, she nodded. "God sends us signs. Be still and listen. Sometimes it's a feeling, sometimes it's a person, but God is always sending us signs." Mia lifted her gaze to meet Logan's. "My dad used to say that."

"He was very smart."

"Yeah, he was. Mom and Dad gave me advice all the time. About school. Life. My faith. I haven't been following any of it." She fisted a hand and placed it in the center of her chest. "There's been a ball of anger sitting right here since they died. It hurts so much."

Logan understood that pain. His own grief swelled and tears pricked the back of his eyelids. "I miss them, too, Mia. More than words can say. I've been trying so hard to be strong for you... maybe that was a mistake. I'm sorry if you felt alone."

Her face crumpled as sobs shook her shoulders. Logan embraced her again, his heart splitting in two. He held her while she cried. A tear or two tracked its own way down his cheeks. The rain picked up speed, drops hitting the window, as if God himself was sharing in their grief.

Finally, Mia's crying tampered off. Logan ripped some paper towels off the roll on the counter and handed them to her before taking another for himself. They both wiped their faces. Then Mia excused herself to wash up and do some homework. She scurried upstairs.

Progress. A small step, but it was significant.

Logan tossed his paper towel in the trash and finished

the dishes. Then he went into the living room. Willow was curled up in the corner of the couch, watching the thunderstorm. Her blonde hair was damp from a shower and she was dressed in yoga pants and a pale gray sweater. She greeted him with a small smile. "Everything okay?"

Logan took a seat on the couch next to her. The scent of her shampoo teased his senses. He placed a hand casually across her folded legs, his palm cupping her knee. Touching her, being close to her, was involuntary. It was also comforting. "How much of the conversation with Mia did you hear?"

"Not much. Once I realized you were having a private discussion, I went to shower."

Of course she had. Willow would never eavesdrop. Logan sighed, leaning his head back against the couch. Exhaustion seeped into his muscles. The wound in his leg pulsed with the thump of his heart. He propped it up on the coffee table to ease the inflammation caused by standing most of the day. "Mia shared her feelings. I think she s processing her parents' deaths, and although it'll be a long road, we're talking. That's a big improvement over where we were a few weeks ago."

"I'm so glad." Willow leaned over and rested her head on his chest. "Mia's very fortunate to have you."

"We're lucky to have each other. She's not the only one holding on to her grief. I haven't been the best model for how to process emotions. It's something for me to work on." Willow had taught him that. Her advice to open up to Mia about his feelings had helped them connect. Logan was grateful. He gently squeezed her knee. "How was the conversation with your uncle?"

"Difficult. He asked if Kathryn apologized. I could hear how much he wants me to forgive her." She sighed. "I keep replaying the conversation with Kathryn over and over in my head. I want to believe she's telling me the truth." She played with Logan's fingers, trailing her own over his. "Is that foolish?"

"No. She's your uncle's wife, and you've known her for over a decade. Seeing the best in people isn't a weakness. It's a gift."

"Do you really believe that?"

The vulnerability in her voice reached inside and squeezed his heart. Logan was tempted to get off the couch, find Mike, and punch him in the face for making Willow doubt her own instincts. "Yes, I do. It allows you to see troubled teens, kids like Mia and Josie, as valuable. You believe in them when others wouldn't." He squeezed her knee again. "You're special, Willow. Don't let what happened with Mike steer you away from trusting your own judgment."

She tilted her head to look him in the face. "You always say the sweetest things to me."

His breath hitched at the look in her eyes. He wanted to drown in those blue depths. Logan brushed a strand of hair off her forehead, his fingers trailing over Willow's silky skin. The pulse at her throat jumped. She pushed up to brush her lips across his. Fleeting, gentle as a hummingbird's wing, but it sent his world spinning. His heart tumbled in his chest.

Logan was tempted to deepen the kiss, but there were things they needed to discuss. His throat closed as the implications of the upcoming conversation stole his breath. Was he ready to tell her the truth about his feelings?

Willow's phone rang before he could utter a word. Logan nearly groaned in frustration.

She answered the call. Her body stiffened with alarm, and then she hopped to her feet. "Okay, I'll be right there." She hung up. "That was Dr. Wrens at the hospital. Josie is asking for me. She's upset and they think my presence will calm her down."

Logan didn't hesitate. "I'll drive you. Let me ask Jason to stay inside with Mia."

He quickly coordinated with his friend. Then Logan and Willow hopped into his Jeep. The garage door rumbled as it opened. Rain beat against the vehicle as he steered out of the neighborhood onto the country lane leading to the hospital. The night was pitch black, the thunderclouds blocking out any moonlight. His wipers worked overtime to swipe the water away.

Logan's phone vibrated in his pocket. Kyle's name appeared on the screen centered in the dashboard. Using the hands-free option on the steering wheel, Logan answered the call. "Hey, what's up?"

"I'm not sure. Remember the email sent to Scott? The one with the photographs of Willow?"

"Yep." He couldn't forget seeing a sniper's crosshairs overlaid on her image. Those photographs were the first threat against her.

"I traced the origin of that email to the Buchanan campaign headquarters."

"Come again?" Logan's hands tightened on the steering wheel as he cast a glance toward Willow. She gripped the handle on the door. Her other fingers were wrapped into a fist. She'd jumped to the same conclusion Logan had. Kathryn had sent the email. "Are you sure?"

"Positive—"

A shape appeared in the road, illuminated by the headlights.

A man. With a rifle.

Logan swerved as gunshots erupted. Pain shot through his left arm. Willow screamed. The Jeep's tires hit a patch of flooded water on the road, and the vehicle thrown off balance by his jerky movements, went into a spin. Trees and pavement flew past.

Adrenaline shot through Logan's body. He desperately tried to maintain control of the vehicle, but to no avail. The tires hit the curb and the Jeep tilted. Logan's seat belt jerked against his shoulder as the world turned upside down multiple times. Glass shattered and metal crunched, drowning out the sound of Willow's screams.

Logan's head hit the side of his door. Pain exploded in his skull.

Then everything went black.

NINETEEN

Everything hurt.

Willow bit back a groan as her body rocked against the hard ground. Her mind was muddled. Nausea threatened to upturn her stomach. Darkness beckoned, but some internal instinct warned her against falling back into oblivion. She peeled her eyes open. Her surroundings were blurry. Haze. Nothing made sense.

She squeezed her eyes shut again and took a deep breath, then reopened them. The ground underneath her jolted and pain shot through her body. She tried to put out her hands to brace herself, but couldn't move them properly. Willow glanced down. She blinked.

Tied. She was tied up. Thick zip ties wrapped around each wrist, binding her hands in front of her.

Her heart rate spiked as the memories came flooding back. The man in the road with a rifle, Logan's vehicle spinning out of control and then flipping, the sensation of someone hauling her through a window and over his shoulder. She'd lost consciousness after that.

Her head pounded with the force of a thousand hammers beating against it. Lifting her bound hands, Willow used her fingers to feel the source of the pain. Something wet coated her skin. Blood. She must've hit her forehead in the accident.

The ground underneath her jolted again. Willow winced and bit back a scream as a fresh wave of agony shot through her left leg. She wiggled her feet. They weren't tied, but her ankle protested any movement. Broken? It was possible. Her gaze swept over her surroundings. She was in a vehicle. A van. The seats had been removed, and she lay on the cold floor. Rain pounded against the roof. Willow tilted her head toward the driver. His dark hair and plain features were unmistakable.

Devon James.

Fear and pain crowded her mind, increasing the adrenaline pouring through her veins. She was alone with a killer. Willow touched her wrist. Her smartwatch was gone. Devon had probably removed it when he'd tied her hands. There was no way for anyone to track her location. Her throat closed as her heart slammed against her rib cage. Dots danced across her vision.

Hyperventilating. She was about to pass out.

Breathe!

The voice broke through her panic. Willow closed her eyes.

Breathe in, hold for two, breathe out.

She kept the rhythm until her heart rate slowed. Freaking out wouldn't help. She needed to keep her wits about her to survive this. Logan would come looking for her...

Logan. Her chest clenched. Was he alive? The crash had been brutal, and the attacker had shot at them before-hand. Tears pricked Willow's eyes, but she battled them back. Negative thinking wasn't the way out of this. Until she knew otherwise, she'd assume Logan was alive. That he —or his friends—would search for her.

God, I need Your protection. Logan needs Your protec-tion. Watch over us both and please bring us back together again.

The prayer soothed her and a warmth centered in her chest. She wasn't in this alone. God would be with her every step, guiding her through, no matter what came.

Where was Devon taking her? Darkness pressed in on all sides, but Willow's eyesight had adjusted to the dim lighting. Beyond the windows, trees whipped past in a blur. They were on a rural road. The vehicle slowed down as Devon braked and then turned. Buildings loomed in the distance. A collection of broken and decrepit old ware-houses. Shattered windows gaped like empty eye-sockets and rust had eaten away at the siding.

The scene looked like something out of a horror movie. A fresh wave of panic stole Willow's breath. She knew with certainty that whatever lay inside those buildings wouldn't be good for her. She couldn't allow Devon to take her inside.

Did he know she was awake? Willow didn't think so. The interior of the van wasn't lit, and with the thunder-storm outside, she was shrouded in darkness. The faint glow of the headlights illuminated Devon's face. His attention was fixed on the road ahead of him.

Keeping as quiet as possible, her gaze swept the interior of the vehicle. It was barebones. There wasn't anything she could use for a weapon. Her mind frantically ran through options, rejecting each one.

Running away when he opened the van door wasn't possible with her hurt ankle. Physically, she was no match for Devon's brute strength. He probably also had a gun. Or two. Despair threatened to drown her, but Willow fought against it. There had to be a way to take him by surprise.

The binds around her wrist cut into her skin. She fingered them, attempting to get relief, when an idea formed in her mind. It was risky. Perilous. But there was no other choice.

Willow kept her gaze on the world beyond the windshield. The warehouses were growing steadily large, confirming that was their stop. Silently, she shifted her body weight, gathering her legs underneath her. The element of surprise was her only advantage. The hair on her arms prickled as every cell focused on the speed of the van and the encroaching warehouses.

Wait for it. Wait...

Devon took his foot off the gas.

Willow shot upward and dropped her arms around his chair. Devon's eyes widened in surprise. In one smooth motion, she thrust the zip tie blinding her hands against his throat and leaned back, using the weight of her body to cut off his air supply.

He gagged. One hand flew from the steering wheel to grab at her arm. Nails scratched against Willow's skin, but she held on as the van weaved. Devon's complexion turned red. Frantic and panicked at the lack of air, he tried to reach for the gun resting on the console.

The van swerved. The weapon clattered to the floor-board on the passenger side.

Willow gritted her teeth and leaned back as far as she could. Choking a man into unconsciousness wasn't as quick as they portrayed in the movies.

Devon clawed at her hands, but his movements grew weaker as his eyes drooped. In a desperate move, his foot slammed down on the gas. He tried to throw Willow off balance by steering wildly. She hung on. The vehicle went into a spin and then the back end slammed against the side of the warehouse.

The bindings around her hands snapped as the force of the crash threw Willow like a rag doll. Her body collided with the unyielding side panel of the van. Fresh pain shot through her entire body. She crumpled on the cold floor, momentarily dazed by the impact, but blinked to clear her vision.

Devon was slumped over the steering wheel. He groaned.

Fresh terror sharpened Willow's focus. She scrambled for the handle to the side door of the van. Agony shot through her ankle when she stood. Cold rain smacked her face, instantly soaking her hair and clothes. Lightning flashed. The bright beam illuminated her surroundings for a precious second. The warehouse in front of her was in better shape than the others. A side door was cocked open. Willow hobbled toward it.

Devon was injured, but he wouldn't stay down for long. She couldn't outrun him in her condition. The best she could hope for was to find a working phone. Or hide until help arrived. Logan and the police didn't know where she was, but Willow didn't dwell on that thought for too long. She needed to put all her energy into survival.

Willow dared a backward glance toward the van. No sign of Devon. She slipped into the warehouse, pulling the door shut behind her. Her fingers fumbled for the lock, but it was broken.

The air was musty and cold. Willow paused, panting, and let her eyes adjust to the dimness. Machinery, left to rot and rust, sat like hulking monsters. Water poured from her clothes and hair to drip on the concrete floor. It left a path in her wake, one Devon could follow. There was nothing Willow could do about that. A sign, hanging from one nail, read office. The arrow pointed to the right.

Goosebumps broke out across Willow's skin as she limped toward possible salvation. The office emerged from the darkness, a square enclosed building in the center of the warehouse. She located the door and twisted the handle.

The room was larger than it appeared on the outside. A counter traversed the full length, the swinging door used by employees to gain access to the back rooms hung on one hinge. Willow limped farther inside, moving as fast as her body would allow. Papers littered the floor. It smelled faintly of urine. Cold air blew in through a hole in the drywall. Someone—a transient, perhaps—had shoved a dirty cloth in the space in a poor attempt to seal it shut. More desks lurked in the rear. There was probably a bathroom back there as well.

Willow scanned the space. An old-fashioned telephone sat abandoned on a filing cabinet. Hope sprang inside her chest. She lifted the receiver.

No dial tone.

Frantically, she pressed a few times on several buttons, but to no avail. Phone service had likely been cut off a decade ago. It'd been a long shot to believe otherwise. Disappointment mingled with a bone-crushing weariness. Her situation was bleak. The storm continued to rage outside. Maybe she should try to escape using another exit and hide in the woods. They were in the middle of nowhere, but come morning, cars might traverse the nearby road.

Plan in place, she set the receiver down. The heading on a sheet of paper caught her attention. The letters were large and bold. JACOBS EXPORTS. An icy chill coursed down Willow's spine. Jacobs had been Kathryn's last name before she married Scott. These warehouses had to be the ones she'd inherited from her grandmother.

The conversation with Kyle in the moments before the collision played in Willow's mind. The email sent to her uncle—the one with the photographs—had been sent from the Buchanan headquarters. By Kathryn? It was the only thing that made sense. Her aunt was behind these attacks.

Logically, it all lined up. And yet something inside Willow whispered there was more to the story. She crumpled the paper in her hand. Logan had urged her to trust her own judgment. Willow didn't believe Kathryn was behind this. She just didn't.

There had to be another explanation.

"Ms. Cassidy?"

Willow whirled. She hadn't heard anyone come up behind her. She squinted in the darkness, but then a match struck and a candle flared to life, revealing a young woman in wrinkled clothes. Recognition took Willow's breath away. "Amber? Amber Miller?"

The last time Willow had seen Amber was two years ago. The troubled teen had lost her mother to drug addiction, and the state took custody of her. There hadn't been any foster homes within Knoxville available, so Amber was moved to a neighboring town. Willow had tried to keep in touch, even offered to drive Amber to the youth center so she could continue participating, but the foster mother had resisted.

Then Amber ran away six months ago. Willow hadn't heard from her since.

"What are you doing here?" Willow took in Amber's clothes and the sleeping bag in the corner of the room. The light from the candle flickered off cans of food and a loaf of bread. "You live here."

"I didn't have any other place to go." Amber took a step back. Fear creased her features. "I won't go back to foster care."

Willow didn't have time to argue that point with her. "Do you have a cell phone?"

Her tone was sharp, and Amber stiffened. "No. Why?" Her attention swept over Willow's body, seeming to take in the blood staining her hair and clothes. "What happened to you?"

A door creaked inside the warehouse.

Devon. He was coming.

Willow's heart skittered. She grabbed Amber's candle and blew it out.

"Hey!" Amber protested.

Willow slammed a hand over the teen's mouth. "Listen to me very carefully." She kept her voice barely a whisper. "If that man finds us, he will kill us."

TWENTY

Willow.

Her name was a mantra as Logan crawled from the wreckage. His left shoulder was bleeding and glass cut into the soft flesh of his palms. In one hand, he gripped Willow's smart watch. Rain soaked his skin, mingling with the blood. Nausea, probably caused by the concussion he'd suffered during the accident, roiled his stomach. It was difficult to breathe, and his chest ached. Broken ribs, maybe? Logan ignored it all.

Devon had taken Willow.

Headlights quickly approached. Tires squealed as a truck whipped to a stop on the side of the road. Moments later, Walker appeared at Logan's side. "Don't move. The police and EMS are on the way."

Logan ignored him. He placed a hand on the twisted side of his vehicle and hauled himself to his feet. His head spun. "He has Willow. We have to go."

Walker grabbed him. "Go where?" Water poured from

the brim of his cowboy hat. His eyes were shadowed and sympathetic. "We don't know where Devon has taken her. You're bleeding." His gaze swept over Logan's shoulder. "You're injured. You can't help her. Tucker is on the way. He'll get every officer in the state to search."

Rage unlike anything Logan had ever experienced pulsed through him. He shoved Walker. "We have to find her." Logan took several steps toward the truck before his body succumbed to his injuries. He stumbled and would've fallen, except Walker grabbed his good arm, keeping Logan on his feet. He tried to shake off the helping hand, but Walker wouldn't let go.

"Stop fighting me, man." Walker's tone was sharp and authoritative. "I'm here to help you. You're a medic, for heaven's sake. What good are you to Willow if you bleed out right here?"

His friend's words cut through the illogical train of Logan's thoughts. He blinked. Training from a decade in the military snapped his mind into focus. The first order of business was to treat his wounds. "Do you have a first aid kit in your truck?"

"Yes." Walker hauled him over to the vehicle and opened the passenger side door. "Try not to bleed too much on the seats."

That last comment was a bit of black humor. Logan grimaced as he lifted his body into the truck. He undid the buttons on his shirt and assessed the wound on his shoulder. He'd been shot. The bullet had traced a furrow along the meaty part of his upper arm. It was nasty looking, but not life-threatening.

Walker got into the driver's seat and popped open the first aid kit. It was well-equipped with pain meds and bandages, along with a powder that would stop bleeding. Logan selected a packet and ripped it open. "How did you find me?"

"Kyle. He called and said you'd been in an accident. I came right here from Willow's house. Jason and Connor are still with Mia." Walker dried his face with a towel, disinfected his hands, and opened a pack of gauze. "What happened?"

"Devon James. Came out of nowhere and shot at the Jeep, which caused us to have an accident. I must've blacked out, because when I came to, Willow was fighting and screaming with him." The memory clogged his throat. "I couldn't get out fast enough to save her."

Walker let out a long breath. "You're not invincible."

"I love her."

The words were out of Logan's mouth before he had time to even process them. But they rang with truth. He loved Willow. Their relationship started out fake, but it'd shifted into something real and meaningful. And she didn't know. He'd been so terrified of telling her about the depths of his feelings, worried about being rejected, that he hadn't given her a chance. Logan hadn't given *them* a chance.

Regret mingled with worry, and pain swirled inside his gut like a hive of bees. Logan couldn't stand the thought of never seeing Willow again.

Please, God, please. Give me the strength and the wisdom to find her.

Walker's phone rang. He handed the gauze to Logan

before snagging the device from the cup holder. "It's Kyle." He answered. "You're on speaker. I found Logan, but Willow has been kidnapped."

"You were set up." Kyle's words were clipped. "I checked and there's no Dr. Wren at the hospital."

Logan gritted his teeth as he doctored his wound. "The phone call was designed to get us out of the house, so Devon could shoot the Jeep and grab Willow."

"Yes. I also know who Devon James is working for. The email sent to Scott came from Buchanan headquarters, and I initially thought it was Kathryn who'd sent it, but then I reviewed the surveillance footage from that day. Mike Jensen sent the email."

Logan's hand tightened on the gauze. "Are you sure?"

"Yes. The email was sent before Kathryn hired him to work the campaign. He's in disguise—dressed as an older man with a beard and mustache—but it's definitely him. Mike used a fake name when he signed in. Everyone must've thought he was a new volunteer. What I can't figure out is why on earth he'd sneak into the Buchanan headquarters to send the email. If he was trying to hide where it came from, there are easier ways."

Logan's mind raced as he considered everything he knew about the case and the threats against Willow. He inhaled sharply. "Mike wasn't trying to hide where the email came from. He wanted someone to figure out it was sent from Buchanan headquarters."

"Why would he want to do that?" Walker asked.

"Because he's planning to frame Kathryn. This is about revenge." Everything snapped into place for Logan.

"What's the best way to destroy Scott? Kill his niece, ruin his political career, and have his wife accused, and possibly even arrested, for murder. The scandal alone would be torture for someone like Scott, who prides himself on honesty and integrity. Mike plans on leaking information to the media. He's built a career by taking down opponents and knows how to destroy someone through public opinion."

"No one will take his word for it," Kyle said. "They'll attempt to trace the originals of the email and discover the same thing I did."

"Not just the media. The police will trace the email too. It'll just take them longer." Logan secured the gauze around his arm. "It's all part of a bigger plan. That explains why Devon kept trying to kidnap Willow. He's taking her to a place connected to Kathryn. They'll kill Willow there." His mind raced. "It has to be remote. Someplace without cameras where there's no danger of them being spotted by accident. Doesn't Kathryn own some warehouses?"

"Yes. They were an inheritance from her grandmother. They're on the west side of Knoxville."

Logan's heart leapt inside his chest as hope took hold. "Send Walker the address. Now."

Walker shoved his truck into gear and hit the gas. Rain pounded against the windshield as they sped through the night. The phone beeped with an incoming text message. Logan tapped on the screen to get directions. They were ten minutes out. He removed his gun from his holster and checked the weapon. It was undamaged from the accident. Logan shoved the magazine back into place. Walker took a turn with the skill of a race car driver. His tires ate up the asphalt.

Eight minutes out. Logan counted the time in heartbeats.

Hang on, Willow. I'm coming.

He prayed they wouldn't be too late.

TWENTY-ONE

The situation had gone from precarious to desperately alarming.

Willow peeked around the office door toward the entrance of the warehouse. Two hushed male voices bounced against the concrete. Then the men appeared. She gasped.

Devon James carried a rifle. His neck was red, his clothes wet and clinging to his skin. Mike was at his side, dressed in a suit, a scowl on his face. Lightning flashed long enough to reveal the gun in his hand.

"How could you let her get away?" Mike's tone was furious. "This is the third time you've failed. What am I paying you for?"

"You told me she wouldn't be a problem," Devon snapped back. "This was supposed to be a simple job. The police are already on my tail. They know I'm involved. That wasn't part of the bargain."

"The cops won't be an issue. I can take care of that." Mike's expression hardened. "Find Willow, but don't shoot her if you can avoid it. I want to be the one to put a bullet in her brain. For my brother."

She inhaled sharply as her blood turned to ice. Mike was seeking revenge. She quickly put two and two together. Kathryn had been right. Mike intended to go to the media, only it was her aunt's good name he would smear. That's why they were in the warehouse Kathryn owned. Killing Willow and framing her aunt for it would destroy Uncle Scott.

The men split up, each disappearing into the shadows.

Willow gripped Amber's hand. The teen was wide-eyed with fright but holding it together admirably. They couldn't stay hidden in the office. It wouldn't take long for Mike or Devon to circle around and check the location. The best option they had was getting out of the warehouse and escaping into the woods. If they made it out unseen, they could hike to the road.

The plan was tenuous with enough holes to drive a tractor through, but it was a fighting chance. Staying meant certain death. That wasn't an option Willow was willing to accept, especially with Amber's life also on the line.

"We need to get out of here," Willow whispered. "Where's the closest exit?"

"Over there." Amber pointed toward the back wall. "There's a door that leads to the rear parking lot."

Close to the woods. It was perfect.

Willow grabbed a rusty pair of scissors from the desk. The makeshift weapon wouldn't help much if Devon and Mike shot them, but she felt better having something anyway. "We stick together, but if something happens, I want you to run and get help. Understand?"

Amber gave a sharp nod, her gaze dropping to the scissors in Willow's hand. "Wait." She scurried across the room and reached into her sleeping bag. When Amber returned, she was clutching a knife. "Okay. Let's go."

They slipped out of the office. Darkness pressed in on all sides. Willow's nerves bundled in her stomach and her heart sped up. She listened for anyone coming their way, but it was impossible to hear over the thunderstorm. The rain beat against the roof in a fiery tempo. Icy wind fluttered the strands of Willow's hair. Fresh goose bumps broke out across her skin.

She gripped the scissors tighter and kept moving. Amber's hand was delicate in hers. The teen was seventeen but malnourishment and stress had eaten away at her youthful vitality. She had to weigh a hundred pounds soaking wet. They offered self-defense training at the youth center, and Willow remembered Amber had taken a class or two, but they were poorly equipped to deal with two killers with guns.

A noise came from Willow's left. She scrambled to hide in the shadows behind a giant piece of machinery, pulling Amber with her.

Devon appeared, using the flashlight app on his phone to search in the dark recesses of the warehouse. Willow sucked in a breath and ducked as he turned in her direction. She held a finger against her lips to indicate Amber should stay quiet. The young woman froze as footsteps drew closer.

Willow gripped the scissors tight enough for them to slice into her palm. The seconds stretched out, the fear so encompassing she wanted to scream. Then Devon's shoes scuffed against the floor as he moved away from them. His light faded.

Amber exhaled. "That was close."

It had been. They needed to get out of there.

Willow rose from the crouch, took Amber's hand once more, and moved toward the door. Her ankle throbbed. Wind snaked through the busted windows, chilling her damp hair and clothes. Every step was taut with pain and terror. Still, she kept moving. Her gaze shifted from right to left, searching the darkness for any sign of the men hunting them.

The door gradually emerged from the darkness like a mirage of hope. Willow picked up her pace.

The air shifted to her right. Mike materialized from the shadows, his gun raised.

Without thinking, Willow rushed him.

Her shoulder slammed into his stomach with the full weight of her body behind it. Mike was thrown off balance. Tangled together, they toppled to the floor. Pain screamed through Willow as her ankle slammed against the concrete. She barely felt it. Adrenaline and a desire to protect Amber raced through her veins. She scrambled to get away from Mike.

He swung out with a fist. It collided with her shoulder and sent her crashing back to the ground. Mike came for her again. Willow reared up, lifted the scissors, and jabbed them into his thigh.

He screamed.

Willow scrambled to her feet. Then she turned to Amber.

"Run!"

The teen bolted. Willow followed, but the tussle with Mike had exacerbated her injuries. Pain shot through her leg from her ankle and her head swam. Something warm dripped down her forehead. Her wound was bleeding again. Nausea threatened to weaken her knees.

Up ahead, Amber slammed into the door and it burst open, spitting her into the thunderstorm. She disappeared.

Something whacked against Willow's back with the force of a train. Her hands shot out instinctively to break her fall as she went flying across the concrete. The air whooshed from her lungs.

Mike stalked toward her, gun in one hand, a metal pipe in the other. Blood darkened his pant leg. His face was pure evil. "I was going to make your death quick, but now... things have changed."

He lifted the pipe.

Willow tried to move, but she wasn't fast enough. Pain exploded across her rib cage. She collapsed. Tears ran down her cheeks and dripped onto the floor. Her mind willed her body to move, but her muscles wouldn't obey. She couldn't get enough air into her lungs.

Mike pulled a cell phone from his pocket. "There's a teenage girl escaping from the west side of the building. Take care of it."

He hung up. Then he crouched down next to her, grabbed a fistful of her hair, and yanked. "You stabbed me."

Her body was bloody and broken, but Willow's spirit wasn't. Mike wanted her to be afraid. She wouldn't give in to him. Not one ounce. She glared up at him defiantly, gathered her courage, and spat in his face.

He recoiled and cursed.

Gunshots outside cut through the sound of the storm. Willow's heart sank. Had Devon found Amber?

No, God. No!

A noise shifted in the darkness. Mike grabbed Willow and pulled her up against him, pressing the gun against her temple. His arms trapped her own by her side like a vise. She peered into the depths of the warehouse but couldn't make anyone out. Everything was hazy. Her breathing was shallow, Mike's arm putting pressure on her ribs, sending waves of agony through her body.

"Who's there?" Mike yelled. "Show yourself."

Walker, gun raised, stepped out of the shadows. His clothes were soaked, his cowboy hat gone, but a steely determination was etched across his handsome features. "Let Willow go."

Mike tightened his grip around her. "No. Drop your weapon first."

Walker smirked. "I drop my gun and you'll just shoot me. That's not happening. Now, the way I see it, you have one choice. Lower your weapon and let her go. It's the only way you walk out of here alive."

"Or I could just shoot her."

"You kill her, I'll finish you before you can take another breath." Walker's tone was deadly cold. "I was a Navy SEAL, Mike. I can shoot the wings off a fly at seven hundred yards. You don't stand a chance." He growled. "Let. Her. Go."

Willow's head spun. She wanted to figure out how to help aid her escape, but her brain was struggling to process information. Everything felt fuzzy and indistinct. Somewhere in the back of her mind, Willow recognized the signs of a concussion. Mike's grip on her chest was crushing, the resulting pain crippling. It was all she could do to keep breathing.

Mike stepped back, dragging her with him.

Then he froze.

"Drop your gun, Mike."

Logan! He was alive! His voice came from behind Mike. He'd snuck in through the door Amber had used to exit. Did that mean she was safe too? Willow's eyes flooded with tears. The staggering weight of her emotions made it even more difficult to breathe. She was gasping for air. Walker shifted position, drawing closer.

"It's over, Mike." Logan's tone commanded authority. "Drop the weapon."

Mike pressed the barrel of his gun against her temple harder. Suddenly, Willow realized he hadn't moved one inch. Logan must be right behind him, a gun to Mike's head. But her ex wasn't in this for money or power. He wanted revenge. To make her uncle pay.

Mike might decide killing Willow, even if it meant he died, too, was worth it.

His hand trembled with indecision.

TWENTY-TWO

Willow emerged from the hospital bathroom, fresh-faced and smelling like lavender. A nurse held her arm to ensure she wouldn't fall. Logan quickly crossed the room and took Willow's other arm to assist her back to bed. Once she was settled and the nurse was gone, he asked, "How do you feel?"

"Tired." She leaned her head against the pillow. Shadows smudged the skin under her eyes. "Who knew taking a shower would be so exhausting? It feels like I just ran a marathon."

"You have three broken ribs, a badly sprained ankle, suffered a concussion, and one of your lungs was crushed. Those aren't injuries you bounce back from right away."

She lifted her brows. "Says the man who was shot, yet stayed here with me all night."

Logan laughed. "It was a flesh wound. Barely counts."

It'd taken dozens of stitches to close the wound, but he'd heal. Physically, anyway. Emotionally, things would take more time. Logan didn't want to think about those harrowing moments after the accident or the sight of Mike with a gun to Willow's head. She'd nearly died several times. Losing her would've crushed him.

A knock on the door preceded Chief Garcia into the room, followed by Scott and Kathryn. All of them appeared rumpled and exhausted.

Scott greeted his niece with a gentle kiss on the cheek. His jawline sported a five o'clock shadow and his shirt and pants were wrinkled. "How are you feeling?"

"Better." Willow gave him a weak smile.

Chief Garcia hooked his thumbs through his belt loops. "I'm sorry to disturb you, Willow, but I thought y'all would like an update on the case. Mike won't see the outside of a prison for the rest of his life. Neither will Devon. Both men confessed to their part in the attacks on you."

Logan breathed a sigh of relief. He'd worried that Mike would lawyer up and drag things out by forcing a trial. Willow would have to testify. It would be a long, exhausting ordeal that would drudge up painful memories. Since Mike confessed, things would be much simpler. "Did he explain why he was trying to kill Willow?"

"It was as you suspected, Logan. Mike blamed Scott for the death of his brother and wanted revenge. He decided to kill Willow and frame Kathryn for it. The goal was to take everything away from Scott, both personally and professionally. Mike paid Bruce Snyder, Willow's bodyguard, and was the one who attacked her in the parking lot."

Willow gasped. "He attacked me?"

Chief Garcia nodded. "Yes. His plan was to kill you in the warehouse so Kathryn would be implicated. When the initial attack failed, Mike hired help. Devon planted the explosive in your car—he learned some basics of bomb-making while in prison—but, according to him, you weren't supposed to be there when the vehicle blew up. They were just trying to make it look like someone was desperate to kill you. Mike wanted Scott to be scared."

Scott's jaw tightened. "It worked. I nearly quit the candidacy half a dozen times." He glanced down at Willow. "You kept encouraging me to stick it out."

"Because you're the best person for the job. The people in this district need someone fighting for them." Her lips curved up. "We're Buchanans. A stubborn breed who don't back down."

He grinned at her affectionately. "True." Scott turned back to the chief. "How did Mike know Devon?"

"Through his brother. Apparently, Samuel and Devon met at a bar and became drinking buddies. After the initial attack failed, Mike promised to pay Devon twenty grand to kidnap Willow and bring her to the warehouse. Devon was given specific instructions not to kill her though." The chief's nostrils flared. "Mike wanted the satisfaction of firing the fatal shot."

Logan's fists clenched. He took a deep breath and reminded himself that Willow was safe now. "Why did they attack Josie?"

"That was Mike. He was furious that Willow had escaped several times and wanted to make her pay. Attacking Josie was an impulsive decision. Thankfully, she's going to make a full recovery."

Logan was glad to hear it. "Who kept sending Willow the text messages?"

"That was also Mike." Chief Garcia rocked on his heels.

"Scott wasn't the only one he was seeking revenge from. Mike wanted to get back at Willow for breaking up with him. According to his statement, she humiliated him. It didn't help when she fought back in the parking lot during the first attack. Mike sent the texts to frighten her."

Wow. The man was unhinged. Logan was grateful Mike would never be able to hurt anyone—including Willow—ever again. "It was stunningly arrogant of Mike to agree to work for Scott's campaign. We wouldn't have suspected him at all if he'd remained in the shadows."

Kathryn's chin trembled and tears filmed her eyes. "That's my fault. I'm the one who offered him the job."

Willow let go of Scott's hand and reached out for her aunt, gesturing for Kathryn to come closer. "It's not your fault. You had no idea what Mike was planning. Besides, he'd already set things in motion long before you hired him." Willow's own eyes shimmered with tears. "Please don't blame yourself."

"How can you be so forgiving after all I've put you through?"

"Because you apologized." Willow squeezed her hand. "We deserve a fresh start."

Kathryn dissolved into tears and gently hugged Willow. Scott looked on, fighting back his own emotions. The tender family moment was the start of a new chapter. Logan was happy for them. Willow had always wanted a better relationship with her aunt.

He pulled some tissues from a box on the bedside table and passed them out. Kathryn thanked him with a gentle smile. She wiped her face. "In the spirit of starting fresh, I called in a few favors. The gala will proceed as planned, although you won't need it, Willow. The youth center has raised all the funds necessary to build the outdoor recreational center."

Willow's eyes widened. "What? How?"

"The chief was kind enough to have a press conference, announcing Mike and Devon have been arrested for the attacks against you and the threat is over. Once that was public, I started making calls." She lifted her shoulders in a small shrug. "Everyone wanted to help. The youth center is an excellent charity. It's easy to fundraise for it."

Willow laughed and then winced with pain. "Well, I may have to steal you away from my uncle once the election is over. Fundraising isn't a skill in my wheelhouse. Neither is party planning, for that matter."

Kathryn's eyes brightened. "I'd be happy to help with either of those. We'll talk details later."

"Deal." Willow shifted her attention to Chief Garcia. "What about Amber?"

"She's fine. Not a scratch on her, thanks to Logan and Walker. My sister is a foster mother and has been for years. Amber is going to live with her. She'll be in excellent hands."

Willow's shoulders dropped. "That's a relief."

"Logan, we have a lot to thank you for." Scott extended his hand. "Consider yourself an honorary member of my family. Anything you need, please let me know."

"Thank you, sir. I appreciate it."

The men shared a handshake. A short time later, Chief Garcia left. Then Scott and Kathryn headed out too. The door clicked shut behind them.

Logan adjusted the blankets around Willow. "Tired? Do you want to sleep?"

"Not yet." She touched his hand. "Would you mind holding me for a while?"

His heart tumbled at the vulnerability buried in her voice. Logan climbed into the hospital bed and wrapped his arms around Willow.

She rested her head on his chest, sighing with contentment. "I needed this."

So had Logan. He threaded his fingers through her hair and gathered his courage. "I love you, Willow."

She didn't move or react. Logan looked down, but he couldn't see the expression on her face. Maybe this was a giant mistake, but he'd already jumped off the cliff. There was no going back. He didn't want to anyway. "Our relationship started out fake, but somehow along the way, I fell in love with you. Your kindness, the way you see the best in everyone, your faith in God. It's beautiful. You're beautiful, inside and out. I want you in my life."

Willow lifted herself up on one elbow. Tears ran down her cheeks. "I want you in my life too."

Hope sprung in Logan's heart. His gaze dropped to her mouth as he swiped at the water on her cheeks. He desperately wanted to kiss her, but there was more to discuss.

Logan hesitated, uncertain how to say this next part. "The thing is, I have Mia. She's always going to be a top priority for me. I won't apologize for it, but it may make things harder for us."

"I wouldn't have it any other way. Seeing how you are with Mia, the way you work so hard to be a good caregiver to her... it only makes me love you more. You're a good man, Logan. The best –"

Whatever Willow was going to say was lost when Logan kissed her. He couldn't help it.

She was everything he could've ever asked for and more.

TWENTY-THREE

Six months later

Logan popped the soft drink can open and took a long guzzle. The liquid was a refreshing burst of sweetness, combating the warm spring day. The sounds of children screaming with joy came from the bouncy house at the edge of the parking lot. Hot dogs, hamburgers, and cotton candy scented the air. Two groups of teens played a spirited game of baseball on the new field. Town residents meandered around the freshly tilled garden. Everyone wore broad smiles on their faces. The grand opening of the Blessed Heart's outdoor recreational center was a smashing success.

The crowd parted, and Logan spotted Willow. Her blonde hair shimmered in the sunshine like liquid gold. She wore jeans that hugged her curves and a Blessed Hearts Youth Center T-shirt. His heart skipped a beat when she turned her gorgeous blue eyes on him. The woman never failed to take his breath away.

Logan closed the distance between them. He kissed her lightly. "Everyone is having a fantastic time. I'm so proud of you."

She beamed, placing a hand on his chest. The diamond engagement ring caught the sun and sent rainbows across his white button-up shirt. "I'm glad people are talking to you about the rec center. All everyone wants to discuss with me is our engagement. How did you propose, when is the wedding day, blah, blah, blah." Her tone was full of laughter, her expression joyful. "I hope you weren't planning on a small wedding."

"Not a chance." Logan took another sip of his drink. "Scott wouldn't stand for it. He's the one who ran the announcement in the newspaper about our engagement. Which, I suppose, is par for the course. You are the niece of a senator, after all."

Scott had won the election last November with double-digit margins. He was doing a stellar job representing the constituents of his district. It was clear he'd started his second career out of a passion to serve his community.

Senator Randall was arrested shortly after the election for hiring someone to threaten the reporter, Ken Watson, and was currently awaiting trial. It wasn't certain he would be convicted, but the evidence against him was strong. Ken had done a multi-week exposé in the paper about the former senator's abuses. It was certain Jerry Randall's political career was over.

Willow's smile faltered. "I'm teasing about having a big wedding, you know. We can have something small—"

"I want what you want." He kissed her nose. They hadn't had a chance to really discuss the matter. Logan had proposed last weekend while having dinner with his family and Mia. "As long as you're my wife, I don't care if we elope or say our vows in front of a thousand guests."

"Hmmm, wife. I like the sound of that."

"So do I." He hugged her tighter.

Willow pushed against his chest. "We're in public. Keep it family friendly."

He laughed. "I'll do my best."

Logan's gaze drifted across the parking lot. Mia was speaking with a group of friends from the youth center. Josie was with them, gesturing adamantly. As predicated, she'd fully recovered from her injuries and was splitting her time between Knoxville and touring with her band.

The teens burst into laughter. It was wonderful to see Mia so happy. His niece had grown more comfortable sharing her grief over losing her parents. She started attending church again and made the honor roll. "Thank you for asking Mia to be your maid of honor, Willow. She was touched."

"You don't need to thank me. I love Mia." Willow smiled. "I want her to be a part of our special day. After all, her life is affected in a big way by our marriage. Things will change. I hope she thinks it's for the better."

"She does."

Willow had approached Mia with genuine openness and let the teen guide their relationship. As a result, Mia hadn't felt pressured. Movies, family dinners, and church had grown their bond. It'd slowly blossomed into a loving and trusting friendship.

Logan smiled down at his fiancée. "Okay, I've monopolized your time long enough. I know you have to mingle.

Would you like something to eat or drink? I could bring you a hot dog."

"Actually, I see Addison in line. Let's go over together and say hello."

They strolled over to the hot dog truck, arm in arm. A few people stopped them along the way, but eventually they made it to Addison.

She greeted them with a bright smile and a hug. "Willow, this is amazing. You've done a great job with the rec center. I really love the gardening section. Nice touch."

"Thank you, but I can't take credit for that idea. It was actually several of the teens who asked to have one."

"Well, you were smart enough to listen to their advice then."

They all laughed. The scent of hot dogs and sauerkraut drifted on the wind. Addison grew pale suddenly and then wavered.

Logan's hand shot out. He grabbed her elbow. Concern coursed through him. "Hey there. You okay?"

"I got dizzy." Addison lifted a shaky hand to her forehead. "I'm sure it's nothing." She swallowed hard, as though she was also fighting back the urge to throw up.

Logan's concern jumped another level. Addison was normally a bundle of energy. His mind ran through several scenarios even as he gently steered Addison to a nearby tent with chairs. He glanced at Willow. "Find Jason. Now."

"No..." Addison objected.

Willow was already gone. She disappeared into the crowd.

Logan pushed Addison into a chair. Then he took her wrist to check her pulse. "Have you had water today? It's warm out." Dehydration could sneak up on a person, although the temperatures weren't hot enough to affect an otherwise healthy woman. "Have you experienced any sickness recently?"

She tried to shake him off. "I'm fine, Logan."

Pulse was normal. He stared into her eyes, checking her pupils. Also normal. "Are you still dizzy? Have you eaten today?"

"I'm fine," she practically growled. "Stop mother henning me."

"I'm treating you as I would any other patient, so don't be so stubborn and answer my questions." As a medic, Logan was trained to consider the most logical reasons for symptoms first, but in this case, he wanted to be sure Addison wasn't experiencing something more serious. This wasn't normal behavior for her. "Have you had anything to eat and drink today?"

Addison sighed. "Yes." She blew out an exacerbated breath. "There's nothing wrong with me, Logan. I'm pregnant."

Surprise flickered through him, quickly replaced by a burst of happiness. He gathered her in a hug. "Congratulations!"

A squeal came from behind him. Logan released Addison, and Willow, who'd returned with Jason and Connor, embraced Addison. Connor's ears pricked up as the woman talked over each other. Willow pressed a bottle of water into the other woman's hands.

"What happened?" Jason demanded, wrapping a protective arm around his wife. "Are you okay?"

"I'm perfectly fine. The smell of the hot dogs did me in,

that's all." Addison drank some water and touched her stomach. "Sometimes I'm starving and other times the smell of food makes me want to run away. We were hoping to keep the news quiet for a bit longer. I'm only ten weeks along."

"We can keep a secret," Logan assured her. He congratulated Jason with a handshake and a pat on the back before petting the German shepherd. "You're going to be a big brother, boy."

Connor's tongue lolled out, and Logan could've sworn the dog was smiling.

Willow laughed. "I think Connor's excited about the idea." She came up next to Logan and looped an arm around his waist. "Your friend group is growing. Marriages. Babies. Pretty soon, we'll be surrounded by pacifiers and diaper bags."

It didn't sound so bad to Logan. He pulled Willow closer. "Will you still love me when I trade in my exciting side career as a crime fighter and become one of those dads that drives a minivan so he can cart the kids to soccer practice?"

Her eyes twinkled. "Yes."

"Promise?"

She laughed. "Promise." Willow kissed him gently. "You make me very happy, Logan. I love you."

He cupped her cheek in his hand and pulled her closer for one more kiss. It was brief but full of promise. Willow was his future, and he was blessed to have her in his life. "I love you too."

ALSO BY LYNN SHANNON

Texas Ranger Heroes Series

Ranger Protection

Ranger Redemption

Ranger Courage

Ranger Faith

Ranger Honor

Ranger Justice

Triumph Over Adversity Series

Calculated Risk

Critical Error

Necessary Peril

Strategic Plan

Covert Mission

Tactical Force

Would you like to know when my next book is released? Or when my novels go on sale? It's easy. Subscribe to my newsletter at www.lynnshannon.com and all of the info will come straight to your inbox!

Reviews help readers find books. Please consider leaving a review at your favorite place of purchase or anywhere you discover new books. Thank you.

Printed in Great Britain
by Amazon